Liberating Tomas

Liberating Tomas

* * *

David Marty

Copyright June 19, 2016 David Marty
All rights reserved.

ISBN: 1534613528
ISBN 13: 9781534613522

I

American beginnings

Claire's evening restlessness persisted, but she finally decided she would try to get some sleep anyway. She was feeling the signals from her body telling her she would be giving birth soon. A full moon night with it's chalky light penetrated the open screened window giving the room an eerily luminous glow; yet it was surprisingly bright. Claire glanced over at Paul blissfully snoring. She was proud of her husband, mostly because he'd dedicated himself to a life of honorable conviction. After all, he was a doctor, even though it was a chiropractic doctor. She contemplated her first six years with Paul, which seemed magical; and laughed to herself as she thought about how he adamantly refused to wash his hair daily because of his ideas about the natural oils and good bacteria of his head helping to insure his health and protecting him from dandruff. Sometimes it s the oddest things that endear another to oneself.

Now in the cool night air, Claire clearly smelled the oily mixture of the strong masculine odors of his hair emanating from the pillow. While she washed the linens every week, Paul's pillow always took on his scent as quickly as she could change the pillowcase. Claire previously gave birth to two healthy daughters and a son. Very soon now, she'd be in labor again. She grew up on the farm so she was very familiar with a cow's disposition when it was ready to calf. Now she was having sympathetic feelings.

As her contractions became more pronounced and rhythmic, she decided it was time to rouse her sleeping husband. Claire reached over and lightly placed her hand on his shoulder.

Paul woke with a startled jerk and quizzically turned to Claire to ask, "Is it time to go to the hospital?

"Yes, I think we'd better get ready," she answered calmly.

Paul quickly got out of bed and used his fingertips to comb back his dark hair. Then he pushed his legs through his trousers. He made most of the arrangements weeks ago and he was relieved. Already, his mother Louise quietly slept in the next room. As soon as he woke her, she'd know to take his place and supervise the remaining girls and boy. Paul bought a brand new shiny Ford in '49, so his car was in top running condition. He'd spent $3.00 to fill it full of gas only a few days ago. He grabbed his shirt from the bedpost. After slipping into his Oxfords and tying them snuggly, Paul helped Claire finish dressing comfortably for the short drive downtown. He looked at his watch and saw that it was only 2:30 in the morning.

It was cool for a summer night in Minneapolis, only fifty-six degrees. The two silently stole away after waking his mother. At the last minute on their way out the door, Claire tossed her green cardigan sweater over her blouse. Traffic was nonexistent because of the hour. In less than fifteen minutes, the staff greeted Claire at the emergency doors and immediately helped her into a wheelchair. Paul parked his new car on the street and wasted no time finding Claire. At Swedish Hospital, most of the paperwork had been finished days earlier. Only a short intake procedure needed completion. Paul's pre-approval gained him access to the delivery room for the birth. At the birth of his first son, two years ago, he assisted in the delivery and ended up fainting. This time, his only task was to observe and coach.

The signals within Claire became stronger and more frequent. Her water broke. The healthy, screaming baby was born after only about an hour, even though, for Claire, it seemed like an eternity. After each birth, Claire always forgot how exhausting and painful birthing was, but the final rewards always made it seem worthwhile. Leaning to natural health principles, Paul convinced Claire that vaginal birth without the new modern painkillers was the best way to have a baby. Claire was not convinced. She didn't always share the same fanaticism about natural health. However, she was young, strong and athletic so she acquiesced to Paul's wishes.

II

Birthday

It was another healthy baby boy. Both Paul and Claire were excited and pleased. Paul and Claire decided on a name for the new baby. It would be Thomas. Paul was especially pleased the baby was a boy. It seemed to balance out the family very well. Paul continued to go to work and back home for the next two days, visiting Claire morning and evening. Against current hospital policy, Claire made a request to have her baby brought to her so that she could breastfeed him. Nursing the newborn was one tenant of health in which that she had total confidence. Then, a few days later, Paul returned to the hospital for the last time to gather up Claire and the baby and they all left the hospital together.

Thomas was born on July 1, 1951. While Truman was still president, the beginning of the long Eisenhower Era was waiting around the corner. The nation was in a post-war boom and unemployment was as low as it gets. Large tracts of farmland and woodlands gave way to suburban residences and shopping malls, not just in Minneapolis but also throughout the entire country. Once Eisenhower took the helm, he launched the interstate highway program, tying the nation together with ribbons of concrete freeways. That program went ahead at full throttle.

Building roads and upgrading them occurred at staggering speeds. The automobile was king and gas prices were low.

Television was just getting its broadcast debut. In the early days, it was primitive, barely a notch above radio. In fact, many early programs were adapted and modified from their radio counterparts. Television would have a profound effect on all American children born after 1950. It was very rare to have more than one television per household. It often sat next to the radio. Television programming became another powerful player in the imprinting of impressionable young minds. In 1951, Tommy was the first generation having television from birth. While his parents were strict about what he could watch, he was able to watch most of the early T.V. shows intended for children.

Thomas was a beautiful baby. Whenever Claire took him out in the stroller, Tommy elicited showers of compliments from the neighbors. However, no one doted on him as much as his two older sisters did. They played with him as if he was their own private doll. By the time he was two, the sisters would dress him in clothes, both his brother's hand-me-downs and their own. Tommy was androgynous and in his younger days, he could easily be mistaken for a girl, especially when dressed in his sisters' colorful garments. He enjoyed all the attention he got and thrived in his family's social environment. Yet his personality had a very sensitive and vulnerable nature.

Tommy wasn't quite two when his younger brother was born. He was hardly aware of the subtle changes that occurred because of his new sibling. However, the two older girls continued their fondness for Tommy, even though the new baby also needed their attention. They continued to play with Tommy as if he were their favorite. When Tommy was almost five, his third sister was born. This completed a family of six children. Paul recorded

Tommy on the brand new, big and heavy, reel-to-reel tape recorder that Claire bought Paul as a gift. The five-year-old could be heard, forever imbedded on magnetic tape, responding very plainly to the question posed by Paul, "Tommy, are you excited to have a new baby sister?"

"No, I'm not. I wanted to have a new baby brother," he defiantly proclaimed.

III

Childhood

At five years old, Tommy was very accomplished in the daily activities of his small world. He enjoyed his role as a middle child. It allowed him a great deal of freedom to lose himself and pursue those things that fascinated him most. Attention seemed to fall first on the oldest sister, then the oldest boy and finally to the perpetual baby, the youngest sister, often leaving Tommy to go unnoticed. At times, he felt left out. However, he learned that sometimes he gained more freedom to explore a more independent childhood when on his own.

Tommy was a very beautiful and handsome young boy. He learned very quickly to capitalize on his good looks when he started school in kindergarten. Most people treated him differently because of his bright-eyed, smiling face and fair features. He learned to obtain power from a mere smile and an inquisitive, sometimes pleading, look at an adult. Tommy also learned that his pleasant attitude was just the ticket to get exactly what he wanted among his peers as well. He was always engaging.

Tommy was very shy and although he knew the power of his good looks, his self-confidence wasn't strong. His family socialization, proved easy; he didn't have to wield any self-esteem to

David Marty

fit into the family. He rarely took on leadership roles so his confidence went untested. Most compliments given to him had to do with how adorable he was, not on his accomplishments. On top of that, Tommy had a difficult time accepting compliments gracefully. He was especially sensitive to criticism. Validation for Tommy didn't seem to go beyond his good looks even in his own family. He merely existed, like icing on a cake.

At five years old, Tommy was already imprinting on his mother, father and siblings to learn how to walk, talk, and mimic behavior. He also imitated the actors of *"Superman," "Leave it to Beaver," "Father Knows Best,"* and *"The Rifleman,"* mimicking behaviors of the movie actors. It was the new audio-visual imprinting, not exactly the same as copying real people, but equally powerful in developing role models and morality in young children who constantly impersonate. Tommy, along with most other children his age, absorbed much of his morality from television and his favorite stars became important role models.

American boys in the '50s were trained to be competitive and aggressive, two qualities, which didn't appeal to Tommy. He admired the girls and their options to wear whimsical clothes of many styles. He also learned to play their games of hopscotch, jacks, and jump rope. He had a gentle tenderness that couldn't equate to the roughness of football and softball. Tommy was also very curious about all the natural life around him, including the life of birds, trees, flowers, animals and even insects.

In all seasons, Tommy played outdoors as often as the weather made it possible. He liked to bike, swim at the nearby lake, and in the winter, ice skate and build snow forts. In the beginning, he stayed close to home, on the same block of his house. He marveled at the different caterpillars and often speculated about what kind of butterfly each worm would transform itself into eventually.

One day, Tommy was home alone with his mom. While Claire washed dishes in the kitchen, Tommy lay on the hardwood floor of the living room. It was raining outside so he wasn't able to play in the yard. He didn't find anything interesting until he moved closer to the fireplace. He carefully watched a parade of small white caterpillars moving from the fireplace toward the outside wall. The parade seemed to get longer as he watched. Finally, Tommy left to find some way to capture the white caterpillars. He ran back with an emptied Band-Aid tin box and he started picking up the fragile tiny white worms with his little fingers and putting them into the metal container. Then he took the box to Claire who was standing at the sink, washing dishes.

He politely asked, "Mom, do you want to see what I've found?"

"Not right now honey, can you wait just a few more minutes?" was her plea.

Tommy was, perhaps, one of the most patient young boys who existed, so he waited. Finally, when he was able to show her his treasures, her reaction caught him unprepared.

"Oh my gosh, where did you get those things? Those are maggots," she shrieked. Her disgust and revulsion overcame her otherwise Pollyanna personality. "Show me where you found them."

Tommy led her to the fireplace where she got on her hands and knees to peer up at the metal damper of the chimney. Then she immediately called the next-door neighbor by telephone asking him to come over. He happened to be home from work. Nathan arrived minutes later and Claire told him of the maggots and asked him if he'd check the fireplace. Sure enough, when he investigated and opened the damper, a rotting dead squirrel dropped down onto the log holder. While the two of them tried to suppress their gag reflexes, Tommy wondered why this part of nature was so reviling to them. He viewed it as just another natural part of the world.

Claire grew up in farm country. Oftentimes in summer, Tommy and the rest of his family spent several days at Auntie Em's and Uncle Rudy's. Tommy loved to watch the young steers and the chickens at the farm. He and his brothers dared each other to urinate on the electrified fences that contained the cows. Aunt Em had the largest garden Tommy had ever seen. Em often commandeered Tommy and his siblings to pull weeds in the immense field. More than once, they encountered a rabbit in the beans. The farm was a home away from city home for Tommy,

Paul couldn't resist a deal. Tommy, about eight years old, learned that Paul agreed to purchase twenty-four chickens at an outrageously cheap price. Paul needed to confront the fact that the chickens were live upon delivery. Tommy and his brothers sat on a log pile and watched Paul chop off the chickens' heads. They laughed with unease as their father sometimes missed and only grazed a beak. It seemed odd that the headless chickens could still run and flap their wings.

IV

Schooling

By the time he went to public school, Tommy had to deal with bullying for being a sissy and ridicule for being a son of a chiropractor (quack). He was a quiet boy who turned into himself and excelled in reading, writing, math and daydreaming. One of his first encounters with older males was during the fire drills when he was in Kindergarten. The youngest students were to line up at the open door when the alarm sounded and wait until the sixth-graders came down in single file from upstairs, each child taking the hand of a younger student. Tommy fantasized he would get to hold the warm hand of an older boy, but during the two drills of that year, both times he got the cold hand of a girl instead.

Tommy had already learned to pretend when his magical thinking and independence seemed threatened in the family. Once in the school system, he used pretending as a cloak to hide his thinking and impulses from his teachers. He was able to portray a programmed boy who always colored in the lines and met the low expectations that all students were to master. While his teachers thought that they had succeeded in conformity, Tommy's thoughts and dreams went well beyond normal.

The 1950s were flush with new cultural icons brought about by Hollywood movies and the technology of television. Children could encounter all kinds of inspiration and fantasies through television and movies. However, one subject was severely restricted during those times; it was sensuality. The media wasn't allowed to film Lucy and Rickie, from *"I Love Lucy,"* in a single bed together, nor could it be shown that Lucy was pregnant with little Rickie. Pregnancy was a hushed and dirty subject. Many other aspects of life were clear; censorship cut out anything to do with sensuality and reproduction.

Initially, to a young boy like Tommy, that wasn't a big deal. However, later on, the absence of sensuality only led Tommy to wonder why sensuality was such a well-guarded mystery. Then he saw movies starring Marilyn Monroe. In movies, she was the first woman that Tom was aware of, to so blatantly flaunt her body's sensuality within the context of the strict movie guidelines in a provocative way. She was unapologetic for her well-developed physique and seemed to capitalize on it deliberately. Tom loved Marilyn because of this, but the sensual mystery continued.

The only mention of anything sensual or sexual from Tom's parents had to do with homosexuals. Usually called queers at the time, Paul and Claire believed queers frequented public bathrooms to first seduce, then abduct and finally to sodomize captive young boys. Claire showed articles to her children that she cut out of the newspapers proving that her beliefs had a foundation in truth. Surely, those perverted men would go to hell when they died. She cautioned all her children that the use of public bathrooms was dangerous. Occasionally, Tommy heard adults snicker and chortle as they whispered to each other about bachelor men living together. Interestingly, two unmarried women living together never seemed to elicit the same consternation.

Another huge imprint in the life of Tommy was religion. Paul and Claire were very religious and took the whole family to church every Sunday. Paul decided that Tommy, out of the three boys, had the best potential to become a minister. Of all the children, Tommy was the only one who seemed to pay attention to the sermons. Tommy felt the heavy burden of his father's dreams for him.

When Tommy went to catechism classes held at the church, he deliberately asked provocative questions about the role of women in the church. The minister sometimes seemed uncomfortable and even embarrassed with his answers. He often verbally stumbled trying to respond. He mumbled something that sounded like, "Women were helpmates but not equal to men." In the earliest years of women's liberation, those words seemed archaic and false to Tommy. He lost his interest in being a minister.

Paul was a chiropractor in the old-fashioned sense. He wouldn't allow vaccinations for his children. At the time, vaccines were new and experimental and Paul didn't want his children to be guinea pigs. Instead, all of his children ended up getting many of the diseases that were supposed to be subdued with vaccinations. However, when they were sick, Tommy's father also nursed his children back to full health with chiropractic adjustments and nutrition. None of them was ever seriously ill. Instead of medicine, Paul taught each child the prayer:

Tender Jesus, meek and mild
Look on me a little child
Help me if it be Thy will
To recover from this ill [1]

---

1 Children's Lutheran Healing Prayer

Tommy imprinted on this prayer, and was especially fond of the part about tender, meek and mild. His impression was the best path for a good boy to follow should be meek, tender and mild mannered. Tommy also formed positive lasting impressions from gazing at the many pictures of Jesus. These became his visual models of male perfection, long hair, slim yet muscular, with a radiantly smooth face, gleaming brown eyes and always a serene and gentle disposition.

Grade school was never very challenging for Tommy. He learned how to blend-in and to answer enough easy questions so that the teachers could hardly expect him to answer the harder ones as well. Tommy was adept at analyzing his teachers and accurately first deducing and then meeting their low expectations.

Tommy learned early on to impress his teachers by overachieving the most challenging topics. In junior high, when the reading assignment was to finish *"Lord of the Flies,"* Tommy decided not only to write a book report, but also to make a three dimensional representation of the deserted island that served as the setting for the book. Of course, Tommy also especially enjoyed reading a book that had wild naked boys running around in it. Throughout his school years, he continually amazed his teachers by his profound thoroughness.

Tommy walked one mile to grade school, rain, snow, or shine. At first, either his older brother or sisters led him by his small hand. However, by second grade, he often walked alone. Tom was curious about his surroundings and sometimes varied his exact route. He liked to pass by a contemporary rambler, which had a pair of wagon wheels framing a long open porch. Tommy was convinced that his heroes, Roy Rogers and Dale Evans, lived there. When he walked home that way, he always hoped to see Trigger grazing in the yard. He sometimes walked that same route with his younger brother and told him, "Yup, this is really the home of Roy Rogers and Dale Evans. I dare you to ring the doorbell!" On the same route, an old gothic style house stood in a dilapidated condition. Tommy often ran by the house thinking that it must belong to a witch who might cast a spell on him if he lingered too long.

Like all American children of the times, Tommy had his flannel cowboy print pajamas. All the boys and many of the girls owned cowboy hats. Tommy even had a holster that he sometimes wore, holding his toy cap gun. Cowboys were usually chasing Indians. After reading several books about early history in America, Tommy became more impressed with the Indians. Of course, he also enjoyed playing an Indian because then he could be almost naked.

V

Growing Up

Tommy was only eight years old when one of his super heroes from television died in real life. It was confusing for Tommy to know that Superman was shot and died. He thought only kryptonite could kill Superman. There was an attempt by many adults to cover up the whole thing. The reported details were meager at the time. The death was a suspected suicide, yet no one was willing to talk openly about it. It was then, after repeated unanswered questions to his mother, and at a young age, Tommy began reading the newspaper regularly so he could get a more accurate perspective on news. It was the beginning of his loss of innocence.

In second grade, Tommy tried to come to an understanding about the mysteries surrounding girls. His first childhood crush was on a girl from his class, Annette. A nice surprise awaited Tommy when his family rented a summer cottage on a lake from Annette's grandparents; she was staying there too. In that one week, Tommy played the role of a husband while Annette played his wife. They had tea and dinner (although imaginary) under a huge old weeping willow tree. They even planned a wedding, which was to be officiated underwater. Girls puzzled Tommy

16

because of their anatomical differences and at his young age, he wasn't sure what those differences really meant. He saw his baby sister naked and wondered, *why are girls' bodies so different and why?* Tommy thought they were missing a most important detail. In addition, *why was there so much shame surrounding nudity?* Tommy felt nakedness was sheer joy.

By the time Tommy reached the third grade, he had forgotten Annette. Now his new friend was a boy. Gary was a smaller, sweet boy, in the same grade as Tommy. Gary's dark hair and gleaming blue eyes intrigued and appealed to Tommy. Tommy wanted to have Gary as a friend so badly that he imposed himself into every activity that Gary loved. It wasn't very long before the two of them bonded. They even shared some after-school activities. It certainly wasn't a sexual relationship at that age. They resonated with each other. After a busy year of friendship, in the winter of fourth grade, Gary accidentally slid under the wheels of a bus and died. The loss was devastating for Tommy. Circumstance took his first real boyfriend from him.

As he grew older, Tommy became even more of a pacifist. He wanted to be kind and nice to everyone. He believed being Christ-like was the ideal way to live. He also believed honesty was always the best policy. Once, when he was at recess, the school bully approached him.

The bully started to nag him and yell in a mocking voice, "Fatty lover, fatty lover. Why do you like fat Philip?"

Tommy being a very sensitive boy wondered why his friendship with Philip, the only fat boy in his class, should be a question. *Why should he be taking a stance?* Tommy wondered. Tommy kept repeating, "Knock it off. It's no business of yours who my friends are!"

David Marty

However, the bully, and now his group of friends, kept pestering Tommy. Finally, one day, as they confronted him, Tommy defended himself by swiftly raising his left knee and connecting hard, directly to the bully's groin. The bully whelped and cried out, running away "dragging his tail between his legs." The boy never bothered Tommy again.

From an early age as most little boys do, Tommy wondered about his penis. He was always interested in comparing his to others. However, he never found himself in a situation where he could even peek at other penises. He had vague memories of his brothers as they bathed together in one tub when they were very young. Now his brothers and father modestly covered their private areas even when they changed clothes. Unlike women's breasts, men's penises always seemed relegated to secrets. One of his first efforts to discover something comparative to himself was to raise the cloak on the small statue of Santa Clause sitting on the bookshelf during Christmas. Santa only had an amorphous bulge where a penis should be. When the Ken doll came out after Barbie, Tommy distracted his sisters long enough to pull down Ken's pants to find another undefined bulge. Because Tommy loved animals, he waited patiently until the huge Sears catalogue arrived each year in the mail. Tommy loved to look at the AKC dogs and various other farm animals available by mail order. However, as he grew older, he used the animals as an excuse so that he could spend time looking at the male models in the underwear ads. Then, only occasionally, he could make out the vague outline for which he was desperately searching. Artwork never showed male frontal nudity. He didn't have a clue then that a penis could get so hard and grow so big as to stand straight up.

One of Tommy's early chores was to go grocery shopping for the family. At first, Claire sent the three boys with their Red Flyer wagon to the Super Value store that was only two blocks away. Eventually, his older brother became busy mowing lawns, so Tommy and his younger brother inherited the weekly task. Sometimes, Tommy had to go alone. His mother gave him a handwritten list and left him on his own to do the shopping. He didn't like it when all the responsibility fell only on himself. Sometimes he had to get help from the checkout woman to interpret his mother's handwriting.

One day, when he arrived home with everything on the list, Claire asked him, "Where are the sanitary napkins?"

Tommy sorted through the brown bags and held up white table napkins wrapped in plastic, and said, "They're right here."

Claire laughed. She explained to Tommy, "Sanitary napkins are the pads that women use during their menstrual periods. They're quite different from regular table napkins."

Another aspect of sexuality that puzzled Tommy; *why did women, need these napkins, but men did not? Why and what was a menstrual period?* Tommy was not so sure that he wanted to know.

VI

Shadow

The summer between fifth and sixth grade, Tom finally got the thing he wanted most for many years. Paul took the children to the Humane Society and allowed them to pick out a puppy. For once, Tom was quite assertive in deciding which young dog he wanted. He soon convinced the rest of his siblings that his decision was the right one. Tom was overjoyed to have a puppy. He lavished so much attention on the dog, which he named Shadow, that the dog became spoiled. It was only a short time later, that Shadow became responsive only to Tom.

The small black dog was part terrier and part poodle. He had the intelligence of a poodle and the tenacity and determination of a terrier. Shadow loved the outdoors. Fortunately, a short white wooden picket fence was just tall enough so that Shadow wouldn't jump it. It didn't prevent him from digging underneath it however. Shadow loved to hunt and bark at the squirrels and rabbits. On two different occasions, he caught and killed unlucky baby rabbits. One day, Shadow tried in vain to get under the fence and ended up severely twisting his neck during the ordeal. Tom heard Shadow's squeals from inside the house and rushed to see what was happening. He freed the dog's head but noticed

Liberating Tomas

the dog's neck remained twisted to one side. Tom took the dog inside and calmed him down by trying to stroke Shadow's wryneck, using the soothing motions of his hands.

Shadow calmed down but his neck remained overly sensitive and he seemed agitated and uncomfortable. When Paul came home from work, Tommy told his dad about the incident. As a chiropractor, Paul knew if the dog's neck remained out of position too long, disease would manifest. Paul adjusted his own children at least once every week until the children were ten years old, making sure that proper alignment of the nervous system would keep their nervous signals strong, which would then keep them healthy. Now, he feared that the misaligned neck of Shadow would cause the young dog to become sick.

The reality of Paul's fears seemed be well founded. A few days later, Shadow began to vomit and convulse. Claire and Tom took Shadow to the veterinarian. Claire was afraid to get near the dog because she could see he was seizing, delusional and might bite irrationally. Tom carefully cradled his dog in a blanket and held Shadow in his arms as he walked into the vet's office from the station wagon. The vet examined Shadow and did a couple of tests, but eventually concluded that the dog had distemper. He strongly supported euthanasia --immediately. Tom began to cry and told the vet that he wanted to take the dog home to his dad.

Paul turned to a chiropractic colleague who had gone through a similar experience with his own dog. He consulted and found a chart of the skeleton of dogs. A phone call instructed Paul how he could adjust the dog's neck and head. With gloved hands, Paul took the head of the dog and forcibly twisted its head until there were several audible clicks. He massaged the neck and injected Shadow with liquid B complex vitamins. Shadow rested more easily that night. By morning, the dog was drinking a lot of water. Paul worked with the dog twice a day for several weeks. As the neck continued to straighten out and strengthen, Shadow began to eat and regain his energy.

Tom was impressed with his observation that alignment was so powerful and necessary for good health. Six months later, Tom brought Shadow back to the same vet. The vet examined the dog and looked up at Tom to say, "I'm so glad that you decided to get another dog. This one's very healthy and will make a good companion for you."

Tom could hardly wait to reply, "But this is the same dog that you saw six months ago and you wanted to put him to sleep. My dad worked on his neck, spine and nerves to bring about a complete healing."

The vet responded, "I've never heard of such a thing in my life. That sounds too good to be true!"

Nevertheless, it certainly was true

VII

Adolescence

Tom's family moved to a newly built house the early part of 1961. At the budding of his adolescence, his new school forced him to begin making friends all over again. It was an awkward challenge for the gentle boy. In sixth grade, at a different school, Tom had his first male teacher, whom he looked to as a possible role model. Tom was first a good student. However, when the students were supposed to be busy with a writing assignment, Tom would steal glances at Mr. Randall. Occasionally, it seemed as if the teacher responded by giving Tom a smile or a nod of his head. A friendly glance back thrilled Tom. Of course, in those days, a teacher could easily lose his job from getting too familiar with a student. Their little silent trysts never went anywhere else, yet Tom felt inspired.

In the same sixth grade classroom, twice a day, boys lined up in one line and girls in another for bathroom breaks. There were only two large bathrooms in this school. Tom couldn't understand the need to rush to the front of the line in order to be first. They were all going to end up at the lavatory. It seemed as if the most insecure children had the greatest desire to be first in line. Tom's goal was to position himself next to Greg, a boy who was

23

David Marty

held-back one grade. Then at the urinals, Tom could peek down at Greg who was only inches away and see what was in store for his own future manliness. Greg's already fully-grown equipment impressed Tom very much.

During the summer after sixth grade, the tabloids reported Marilyn Monroe had taken her own life. Tom was in love with her and felt his role model for sensuality had abandoned him. Her death deeply moved him. He was now on his own. He wanted to carry on her mission of unapologetic sensuality. Tom was pleasantly surprised when he found out that in her real home, she preferred to walk around naked. If Tom lived alone, he would walk around naked too. For Tom, she added a refreshingly candid sensuality to her movies.

Tom was now even more curious in discovering the secrets of sensuality because of the mystery that enshrouded sex. By the seventh grade, Tom was on the verge of puberty. However, he remained naïve and uninformed about the whole subject. From his older brother's friends, Tom overheard things that he figured had to do with sexuality. One such story overheard, if a boy played with and stroked his penis long enough, a white gooey liquid, similar to Ivory dish soap, would shoot out. Tom didn't have long to find out about the truth of the story. One night in the wee hours of the morning, Tom woke up from a wet dream with gooey liquid all over the sheets and his erect penis throbbing. His penis felt more alive than ever before. Many times after that, he locked himself in the least used bathroom at home so that he could perfect his masturbation techniques. Tom wondered why an orgasm felt so incredibly good. Then he began to experiment to see how often he could repeat such an enjoyable feeling.

Sex conflicted Tom. There seemed to be a shroud of shame around sex. Open talk was not tolerated. Tom finally realized why there was a difference between men and women sexually, yet he was supposed to be eager to explore women and then hold them in total honor, never to sexually violate them until marriage. However, most of the popular boys and girls were already fooling around sexually with each other. Then there were the most monumental sensations from when he masturbated. The activity left his whole body energized, re-awakened, and moved to a higher plain. In art, painted women often had exposed breasts that seemed excited and fully plumped, but men with excited penises were restricted to pornography. America severely regulated and prohibited pornography. A person would think that sex organs should get an honorary role of pride of sensation and reproduction.

In seventh grade, Tom was in math class when an announcement came over the loud speakers. A wounded President Kennedy died. That incident ushered in a darker side of government that began to introduce cynicism into Tom's ideas of authority and further accelerated his loss of innocence.

Junior High was the first time Tom had the opportunity to see and walk around with other naked boys in the showers after gym class. After the required gym class, the boys stripped down naked, putting their gym clothes in their lockers and proceeded to the common showers. Some of the boys previously belonged to the YMCA and were accustomed to being nude in the showers and the swimming pool. For Tom, it was the first time that he could actually look at other boys who were completely naked. It became his favorite part of gym class. When other boys' penises became stiff, particularly the boys who were the most mature, Tom's peripheral vision would slyly drink in all the visuals and vicariously swallow the wondrous erections. He enjoyed being a

David Marty

voyeur. However, it was also the time of his life when without any advance warning, Tom might sprout his own erection. He liked to wear pleated pants in class because they offered him some degree of camouflage. Having an erection in class, especially in gym class showers, was an invitation for teasing.

Because of peer pressure, Tom decided in the ninth grade, that he should consider dating a girl. Tom loved to dance and he was good at it. His sisters, as well as *"American Bandstand,"* taught him all the latest dance moves. One day at an after-school dance, he got up the courage to ask Cindy if she would dance with him. The honor was Cindy's that such a handsome boy would ask her to dance. It wasn't long afterward that they began to date. What that really meant was Tom walked Cindy home from school. Then, they spent some time watching television in the basement of Cindy's house, while her mother was busy upstairs cooking dinner. Tom never really knew what else he was supposed to do with a staunch Baptist girl. Allowed or not, rules dictated behavior. While holding hands one day, Tom noticed that Cindy's thumbs were strangely truncated and on one of her thumbs, she had an unsightly wart. It proved a turn-off and gave him an excuse to avoid further close contact. Tom took Cindy to the big formal dance at the end of the year. After ninth grade, he and Cindy drifted apart.

In high school, his definition of his body and progression to his manhood accelerated. Tom observed the boys with the nicest legs and rear ends were the boys who ran the high hurdles in track. He deliberately joined the track team, determined to develop a beautiful physique. At the peak of his years for forming muscle, he ran the high hurdles and worked hard to develop a sculpted derriere. He expected another bonus might be to live out the fantasies he dreamed of while taking showers with the

Liberating Tomas

team. It happened that the older and most beautiful young men on the team were in their own cliques and Tom, more often than not, took showers alone or with less appealing boys his own age after track practice.

Even in high school, Tom was still shy and not well socialized. Rather than try to become a member of a clique, he retreated into his own world. Not being popular, Tom didn't have to confront the sexual complexities of dating girls. He joined a Classic Book of the Month Club, read the daily newspaper, and did his homework. Tom didn't participate in after-school activities. In twelfth grade, he began work at Sears in the catalogue sales department. At that point, he no longer had any extra time for socializing. Tom went to the annual Sadie Hawkins Dance because a girl asked him to go. However, he skipped the prom because it would have cost too much of his hard earned money and he didn't have a girlfriend.

Tom learned very early on, in his public schooling, how to pretend that he was "normal" and on the same page as every other child in his classes. It was easy for him to comply with his teacher's mediocre expectations while at the same time cloaking his magical thinking that took him to all the worlds that he witnessed in his extensive readings and television programs. Always the dreamer, he used his thinking to engage his world without the bias of programmed attitudes.

VIII

University

Tom decided to attend the University of Minnesota mostly because he felt that he'd be able to find other men more like himself. There had to be others who were neither "queers" nor child molesters, but just enjoyed being naked with other men, who were unashamed of sharing erections while pleasuring one another. He was desperately seeking validation as a person and as a man who loved other men. The first year of university, he worked at Sears in the evenings and lived at home with his religious parents. There was little time to meet anyone. Tom decided his best chances to meet another person similar to himself was by hitchhiking to and from work and school. The rides never amounted to anything sexually suggestive, a huge disappointment to Tom. His only recourse was to relieve his sexual tensions alone, by himself.

He attended classes, which sometimes had up to two hundred or more students in them. Tom liked to find an early seat in the large auditorium and watch other male students as they arrived. He fantasized about some of the more handsome young men and visually stalked them through the semester. Tom had fantasy relationships with several young men even though he was always too shy and scared to think about directly approaching any one of them.

During the second semester at university, Tom was in the student union hall when he spotted a notice posted on the bulletin board for charter flights to Europe. He wondered if foreign travel might be a better way to find someone else who had his same inclinations. Tom became obsessed with thoughts of discovering his true sexuality in Europe. Maybe he could convince his parents to allow him to go to Europe alone. Nevertheless, he needed a plan so that he would also seem sincere about going to Europe for cultural enhancement.

Tom excelled in French while in high school and was currently taking French at the university. It certainly would be to his advantage to spend some time in France immersing himself in the language. He plotted, planned, and found a French work-study program based on archeology. It was open to young students under twenty. The program was mostly for French students but Tom got his first passport and began to fill out papers to join the French archeology club. Then he bought *"Europe on Five Dollars a Day,"* by Frommer. There were all kinds of low cost ideas on travel, including lists of campgrounds. For many students of the time, European travel was the thing to do in the summer.

Tom amassed a sizeable bank account by working two years and he figured he could go to Europe and spend $3.00/day average if he hitchhiked and camped and worked in France for a month. Of course, Tom planned to bring more money just in case of emergencies. His strategy of how to broach the subject to his parents took weeks of planning.

Finally, when both Paul and Claire were home at the same time, Tom decided to ask permission. He opened quite formally with, "The University is sponsoring charter flights to Europe for

David Marty

the summer. I would like to go there as part of my studies. I already have an offer to work in France for a month. It would be an educational experience to go to Europe for three months this summer."

"But how would you be able to pay for it? Would you be able to have enough money to pay for next year's tuition? Traveling can be very expensive." They both seemed to be alluding to the same curiosities. "What kind of job is it in France and how much would they pay you?"

Tom answered, "The job in France is a four weeks commitment and they don't pay me, I pay them $10.00 a week. However, I get room and board for that. I'm planning to hitchhike and stay in campgrounds most of the time, maybe take a train once-in-a-while, and I have the book *"Europe on Five Dollars a Day."*

His father responded, "You can't live in Europe on five dollars a day."

Tom countered, "The book says that I can."

Claire sounded worried when she asked, "Is it really safe to hitchhike all over Europe? They're having riots in France, just like students are rioting and being shot here in America." Then she actually said it, "I'm worried about your safety, and what if you got sick over there?"

Tom responded, "I feel that I'll be just as safe and healthy there as I am here. I'm eighteen years old and I don't really need your permission, but I would appreciate your blessings."

They looked beaten but finally, they agreed that if Tom thought he could manage it financially, they would allow him to go on his journey. Tom was relieved. He really wanted to go to Europe to widen his studies. He also wanted to get answers to the questions about his sexuality. He was still a virgin and not really convinced that he was queer.

Nineteen hundred seventy was a time of social upheavals, war, hippies and student protests in the United States. The U.S. was still fighting a brutal civil war in Viet Nam and suffering sobering and traumatic defeats at the hands of guerilla fighters. Students were protesting and rioting against the escalation of the war and bombing of Cambodia. Hippies were opting out of the mess by creating a sub-culture of communal living, free love, and marijuana smoking. Congress reinstated the draft because volunteers were not as plentiful and as eager as the military had hoped. Students were no longer going to be automatically exempt from the draft and they were protesting on the university campuses. On May 4, 1970, at Kent State University in Ohio, National Guardsmen opened fire on a small group of unarmed protesters, killing four students and wounding nine.

This incident led to a national student strike by four million students. Tom's choice to enter the fray came after many of his classes were suspended. During student protests on his own campus, police herded many students, including Tom, into a large open mall at the university. Pepper spray and tear gas caused Tom to resent authority. The war in Viet Nam continued and allowed people to see much of the fury of the conflict on the evening news. Tom personally experienced police atrocities at his own school that year.

Two years earlier, marked the assassination of Martin Luther King Jr. on April 4, 1968 followed by the assassination of Robert Kennedy in June. The landscape had become much more violent and frightening since the era of Eisenhower. Innocence seemed to be lost for the country although it was not totally lost for Thomas.

While discouraging, Thomas retained most of his youthful pragmatism and didn't accept many of the fearful attitudes that

David Marty

seemed to entrap the rest of the nation. Optimistically his focus was on finding out who he really was and how he fit into society, being a contributor for the better good. He was always curious and hoped to find insight to the perplexing dilemma of his sexual identity. Since 1969, Thomas read about men like himself, who rose up to fight for gay rights at Stonewall, in New York. If Thomas decided he was gay, maybe he'd have to join the struggle and fight to get the same rights afforded to straight men. Thomas didn't think it would be possible for him to live a life of secrecy forever. It was in this background that Thomas decided to take his sabbatical in order to establish some rational plans for his future.

Across the pond, 1970 was also a year of change for the Iberian Peninsula. The dictator of Portugal, Antonio de Oliveira Salazar, would die in July. Generalissimo Francisco Franco of Spain was old, ailing, and holding power in name only.

IX

Flying

The time finally arrived. Tom saved his money, paid for his round-trip charter flight, and organized himself for a three-month tour of Europe. He bought a huge canvass Duluth backpack at an Army surplus store, which was drab Army green and frameless. He also bought an old fashioned, very heavy, canvass pup tent because nylon tents were not readily available. Tom's parents' best friends, June and Harry gave him a tin mess kit with an aluminum pan and some cooking utensils including a fork, knife, and spoon. He added a paperback novel and the Frommer book for reference. Tom bought a harmonica for his own entertainment, which proved to be a wise move on his part. He decided to bring only a few changes of clothes and a sweatshirt and light jacket. He purchased a new 35mm camera and some boxes of high-speed color film.

The strategically packed backpack of everything he was taking weighed about fifty-five pounds. Tom only weighed 140 pounds and it took Tom all his strength to sit down, pull the leather straps across his chest, and get back to balance on his feet. He practiced many times in his parent's living room. He'd joined the French work-study group. Tom agreed

33

David Marty

to work in the "club" for four weeks, wherever they assigned him. When he got his assignment, he learned it was to begin in Lavardens, France, starting in late July. Beyond that, his trip was unstructured and Tom was going to land in London to begin his journeys. Then he was free as a bird to go anywhere his heart desired.

This was going to be an adventure that would indelibly imprint Tom's character. He was looking forward to seeing the world. His life had been sheltered and protected to this point. Tom would turn nineteen during his trip. He still lived at home with his conservative parents. He was still a virgin, sexually, and green behind the ears socially. Although very shy, Tom was determined to reach out to strangers and engage in conversation. Tom attended one year of school at one of the largest universities in the country. Now, he had to overcome his passive shyness and steel himself for the realities of many different cultures and every type of people. He was affable and carefree with an adventurous nature. Tom was ready for this bold new adventure.

Camping had never been Tom's strength. In fact, he never camped in a tent before. His parents didn't allow Tom to join the Cub Scouts or Indian Guides. He wasn't sure what life alone at night in a tent would be like. He slept a few nights in the backyard ahead of his departure and felt comfortable with it. He was a Cancer and traveling with his self-contained home appealed to him.

Both his mom and dad drove him to the MSP international airport. Tom's parents said their goodbyes at the boarding gate. All who were flying on the international flights were required to be there early, so there were many other anxious students and faculty milling around. Tom didn't understand why, but

34

Liberating Tomas

for unknown reasons, the most obese, insecure student of the group who was a total stranger, approached him and asked Tom if he could sit with him on the long flight going to London. Tom wasn't good at saying no, so he agreed that he'd sit with Bill on the plane. Tom found Bill to be a heavy, out-of-shape young man who seemed immature and spoiled; not the type of friend that Tom would've chosen. Bill reminded Tom of someone who would be unable to appreciate cultural variations of Europe. It was both Tom and Bill's first plane ride.

After the two of them found their seats on the plane, Tom realized that Bill was determined to intrude into his solo dreams. Chaperoning a childish and frightened young fat man was not going to be very fun for Tom. Tom began planning his method of detachment from the situation even as the jet was getting airborne.

Tom was amazed that there were so many people on the plane. Nearly every seat was full. In those times, all passengers who chose to smoke cigarettes could do so in their seats. Many did. However, Tom didn't smoke. Fortunately, Bill didn't either. He turned down the flight attendant's offer for cigarettes, wine or cocktails. Bill was feeling homesick from the moment the plane left the runway. Tom busied himself by closely observing the various students and teachers sitting on the plane, flying off to Europe. People watching always intrigued Tom.

Tom felt exhilarated by his impending freedom. It was a long flight and Tom sometimes read his book, sometimes dozed off, but was frequently brought out of his reveries by Bill asking questions, wanting something, or needing attention. Near the end of the flight, the plane flew over the emerald green island of Ireland, energizing many of the passengers. Tom was excited

David Marty

because he'd soon be in older and more established cultures. He was anxious to get to London and start his adventure. He was also sure, now with his family far from him, that he would be able to explore his sexuality without encumbrances. Tom looked out the plane windows and saw quaint thatched cottage roofs near Heathrow while the plane was descending. When the plane finally landed, Tom thought, *how nice, at least here they would be speaking English.*

X

Arrival in England

Tom was very surprised to find out that British English was a very different version of what he was familiar with; it took his whole concentration to enable him to understand it. After landing at Heathrow and clearing customs, the two young men boarded a bus that delivered them to central London. All the time zones they crossed distorted their time reference. Tom thought it was early morning; it was actually midafternoon, London time. They noticed a Bed and Breakfast with a vacancy sign posted in the window. They registered with the host and then both of them unpacked some of their things in the tiny room and tried to get their bearings. Each slept a little, but their body clocks were all out of sync. In the early evening, Tom and Bill walked around the area they were staying in and had a bite to eat. They traded in some dollars for pounds and schillings at the airport, which they were just now becoming familiar with spending. Bill was whinny and unhappy that his favorite foods, such as hamburgers and Coca Cola, didn't appear on menus. Tom was eager to try almost anything foreign.

Early the next morning, looking out the window, Tom saw horse-drawn delivery carts, some with dairy and others with

David Marty

fresh garden vegetables, right in the middle of London! Bill and Tom, together, stumbled down the steep narrow stairs to the kitchen where their host served a hearty English breakfast of tea and cream, eggs with sausage, and boiled potatoes. The two of them only spent one night at that bed and breakfast. The next day, they found another, which was also on the second floor, but hugged a lower ethnic Indian restaurant. The strong aromas of exotic curried cuisine were enough to drive Bill to plan an early departure for France and Tom had to work hard to conceal his delight of seeing him go. Tom finally found himself on his own.

Neighbors in Minneapolis were originally from Great Britain. They'd advised Tom, if during his trip he were to get sick or injured, he should attempt to get back to Great Britain for free medical care. A sister of theirs was a barrister in London, and they had parents who lived in Wales. Tom promised to visit and connect with all of them. After several attempts to locate the sister by telephone using the red outdoor phone booths, he finally was able to reach her. He met Molly. She treated him to lunch, and told him tales about her life in London.

Tom went off on his own and saw Big Ben, The Changing of the Guards at Buckingham Palace, Madame Toussaud's Wax Museum, and Hyde Park. It was interesting for him to see horses in the park in the midst of urban civilization. Centuries-old trees towered overhead. It was a clear, sunny, and warm afternoon, apparently rare for London in June.

As was said before, Tom's parents taught all of their children to refrain from using public restrooms unless necessary. However, while in Hyde Park, Tom had a call of nature and the only nearby facility was a public restroom. He hesitantly entered the men's side. It was a small brick facility with a couple of urinals and two toilet stalls. It had a wooden floor constructed of

38

wide planks. Tom rushed into a stall and checked to be sure, there was enough toilet paper. There was. Sitting on the toilet seat, he couldn't help but notice a large round cut out hole been between the two stalls. He'd never seen such a thing before. He felt vulnerable, without privacy. He was soon finished with his business when a slightly older man, in his late twenties, entered the other stall. Tom wasn't sure if he was supposed to avert his eyes, but he couldn't help himself and peeked through the hole in the wall separating them. The young lad noticed Tom looking at him; then he encouraged Tom's attention.

Tom watched as the man pulled down his pants and exposed a beautiful, long, uncut penis. Then he started stroking it and it got even bigger. Tom watched in total amazement. He'd never seen another man playing with his penis in an aroused state. It was truly magnificent. It was mesmerizing. Tom was very fascinated. The young lad's penis appeared much larger than Tom's. This man was clearly putting on a show for Tom, so Tom put one eye near the hole in order to embolden the British man and encourage his exhibition. While enjoying the entire scene, Tom suddenly realized that this man could be one of those perverts of whom his parents had warned him. Tom shivered with the thought about the next thing the man might try to do is to sodomize him. Being impaled on such a large penis was a horribly frightening idea, yet strangely erotic. Tom remembered the visits to the vet, for his dog Shadow, and thought about how inserting a cold anal thermometer always triggered an erection in his dog.

After seeing almost all he could see, including a final incredible orgasm, Tom abruptly got up during the man's afterglow and fled the restroom. The Brit quickly followed him and Tom became increasingly fearful. He walked as fast as he could along the sidewalks toward his room with the Englishman tight on his heels. He didn't want to draw attention to himself by running. Then, Tom began to think, *if I go to my lodging directly, the Londoner would know exactly where I was staying.* Tom tried to elude him with evasive maneuvers, in and out of shops, and up and down streets. Finally, after more than an hour, he was sure that "the pervert" had given up the chase. He was safe; now if only he could remember where his Bed and Breakfast was located.

When he was back in his room, he thought about the exhibitionist and wondered how it might feel to stroke his penis. Maybe the man wasn't a molester at all. Maybe this was exactly what Tom had come to Europe for. Tom dreamed and fantasized about that beautiful penis and stroked himself to sleep that night and many nights afterward thinking about the man.

London 06-16-70

---

2 © Sylvaindeutsch/Dreamstime.com-London Big Ben Photo

Dear All;

I left London yesterday and hitchhiked to Bridgend in Wales. Then I took the bus to Laleston and am at Dr. Quinn's parents' house now. It's raining now, the first since I got to Britain. I will stay here a few days and then go to the coast or to Scotland. Unfortunately, I don't think I'll have time to come back here, so you won't be able to call, as this card will get to you in four to five days from now.

Love, Tom

XI

Hitching

The next day, Tom decided to begin his hitchhiking adventure. The plan was to hitchhike to Wales to visit the neighbor's (from Minneapolis) parents. It was going to take all the courage that Tom could muster to head off to new adventures in a foreign country and engage with people who were complete strangers, from different cultures and sometimes speaking different languages. In only a few days, Tom had begun to realize that in Europe, there were many variations of attitudes and lifestyles. Tom took the Tube as far west as it went and then found the roundabout connecting to the main highway out of town. His apprehension was high.

Tom wasn't the only hitcher on the road. Sometimes, especially leaving the London core, there were queues of up to fifteen youths waiting for a lift. The best place to catch a ride was at the roundabouts. While he waited in queue, he'd take out his harmonica and try to play a few tunes. He was surprised that a driver pulled up to him far from the head of the queue and open the passenger door to let Tom enter.

"Why don't you play a few songs for me," the middle-aged man said. "What songs do ya know?"

42

Tom had only played his harmonica a few times and his repertoire was limited. He obliged the driver with "*Oh Suzanna*," and "*God Bless America*." Often drivers would stop exclusively for him because of that harmonica.

Of course, traffic moved in the opposite direction, drivers keeping to the left; steering wheels were on the right. Several times, in the beginning, Tom approached a stopped car that was waiting for him and tried to get into the driver's seat. Once he even got a ride in a sidecar attached to the left side of a motorcycle, which was an interesting novelty. That arrangement didn't allow for conversation because of the noise and the wind blowing through his ears. He laughed to himself when he finally realized that Way Out was not a huge suburb with multiple ways to get there, but only an English term for Exit.

By nightfall, he made it to Bristol. He contemplated *what a busy and interesting first day of hitchhiking.* Thoughts of the Beatles and their beginnings went through his mind. He hadn't started his tent camping yet, so Tom found a room to sleep for pocket change. The second day proved to be more difficult. He got a ride to the border of Wales, but rides were fewer and farther between. Tom was just starting to realize distances and to comprehend the time it might take to travel from point A to point B. It was often unpredictable and depended on the isolation of the road and the amount of traffic on that road among other things. Isolated roads had fewer vehicles and quirkier drivers. Busy roads offered the dilemma of how to get drivers to slow down and stop. The lorry drivers were most often the ones who picked him up. Many of them were lonesome and appreciated the conversation. Each new ride was a rich new and different encounter. Tom was near Bridgend when the last truck driver dropped him off, late in the evening. His slow progress that day disappointed him.

David Marty

While stepping out of the lorry through the heavy mist, Tom could barely make out the lights of a local pub in the distance. That evening, cold water particles hung in the night air causing a thick and shrouded fog. Tom felt as though he was in the middle of a Dracula movie. He couldn't see more than three feet in front of him. He was at the outskirts of a very small town, after eleven at night. As he walked closer, the fog seemed to part and he was able to see the sign on the pub that also announced, "Rooms to let." Tom didn't want to wake the parents of his back-home neighbors at such an hour, so he asked the proprietor, "Can I get a room for the night?"

"Of course you can. Have you been travelling far?" the proprietor asked.

"I started out this morning from Bristol. It's been slow going."

"Sorry, traffic isn't very heavy in these parts."

The wife took Tom to an upstairs room and made up a bed for him. She looked at him and said, "You look terribly tired. Would you like some warm food before you retire?"

"No thank you so much," he replied. Tom was too tired to eat. The bed was clean, but because of the cool humidity, the heavy white cotton sheets felt damp and clammy.

The next morning, Tom called the Quinn's on the telephone. Mr. Quinn answered and instructed, "Tom there is a bus that runs from where you are to our town. I think it stops there at 10:00. Get on the bus and be ready to get off again at the next stop. I'll drive over to pick you up."

Earl was waiting in the car when Tom arrived by bus. "I was expecting you yesterday," he said. Then introduced himself," I'm Earl, David's father."

44

Liberating Tomas

Tom took a quick survey of the older, white-haired man who was quite fit and trim for his age. "Good to meet you, Sir", he answered.

Within a few minutes, they arrived at the stone cottage, where Edna was waiting. Mr. and Mrs. Quinn were wonderfully generous. Edna offered, "You must be hungry, Please put your bag in the spare room and I'll start breakfast."

They acted like grandparents that Tom never had. Their stone cottage was cozy and comfortable. A small stove kept the dampness to a minimum. Mrs. Quinn offered huge meals to Tom at lunch, dinner and breakfast because she thought he was too skinny.

At the first meal, Edna noticed that Tom didn't use his eating utensils properly. She commented, "Dear, if you plan to travel to the continent, you'll have to learn some new table manners."

Therefore, she began teaching him how to eat continental style, fork in the left hand and knife in the right. The hardest thing for Tom to learn was to balance peas on a fork turned upside down in his left hand, and get them to his mouth without dropping any. They watched television in the evening, mostly news and British comedy. Tom stayed with them only a full day and night and left the following morning.

The next morning, Edna was outside sweeping the cobblestones. She stopped to pick huge snails off the lush dewy vines that grew on the short stone walls. "These little devils will eat everything in sight if you ignore them," she mumbled to no one in particular.

It was such an idyllic scene. Summer flowers were in bloom everywhere. Tom was anxious to get on with his trip. After a hearty breakfast, Edna was confident that Tom could pass his eating etiquette. Tom gave a last hug to Edna. Then he said to her, "Thank you so much for the wonderful hospitality and all the good food."

Earl drove him to the main road that led back to England. Along the way, he pointed out the old grassy, treeless mounds that used to be coalmines and now had grazing sheep on them. When it was time to get out of the car, Earl told him, "Have a wonderful journey, keep your wits about you and most importantly be safe."

Blackpool 06-26-70

Dear Mom and Dad;
    I left Wales this morning and headed for Scotland. I hoped to make it in one day. Now I 'm staying at Blackpool on the

---
3 © Tommason/Dreamstime.com—Blackpool Tower Photo

Liberating Tomas

west coast of England. I'm camping for the first time—only three shillings ($.36). I hope it doesn't rain, it seems like it won't. This will probably be the second card you get today. I'll leave for Edinburgh tomorrow afternoon. The lorry drivers have been great in giving me lifts.
Bye for now, Love, Tom

XII

Blackpool

Once on the main road, Tom decided that he'd enjoy going to Scotland. He headed north, traveling through Birmingham, Stoke on Trent, Manchester, and Preston. One of the lorry drivers suggested spending the night in Blackpool. By nightfall, he arrived at Blackpool. Tom found a campground that cost $.36 for the night. Blackpool was supposed to be the Coney Island of England. It had a beach (freezing cold water!), Ferris wheel, and amusement rides. There was a carnival atmosphere--though very understated, as the English often seemed to be in general. This was an unplanned stop but proved interesting.

The campground was old, and seemed as if it was from another era. It had ancient, yet very sturdy, porcelain toilets and urinals. The showers were cold water, unless you came prepared with coins with which you could buy hot water. Because Tom arrived late in the day, he found himself all alone in the men's large group shower and could only wonder, *if all the showers were in use, would it be similar to his shower days in junior high school?*

Hitching north from the Midlands was a challenge. Mostly, Tom got his rides from more lorry drivers heading north. He got rides to Carlisle, and Abington. The weather was damp with

48

intermittent rain. After two full days on the wet roads from Wales, he eventually made it to Edinburgh. Tom found a wonderful campground, high on a ridge, overlooking the Firth of Forth. He spent three days at the camp and every day he rode the bus into town. He was relieved to have a few days off from traveling the road. It was a welcome change of pace. Sometimes, hitching could be lonely and tedious.

Castle of Edinburgh 06-28-70

Dear Sis, Hope you had a happy birthday. I'm staying in Edinburgh, at a campground, and will be leaving tomorrow. I bought a sweater here because it is so cold. It's been raining quite a bit but my tent isn't leaking. Hope you are all well. I'm fine even though I've been drinking the water. Say hi to Shadow for me. I am sending a long letter soon.
Love, Tom

XIII

Edinburgh

This campground was much more modern than the one at Blackpool. As in most European campgrounds, the spaces were tightly packed and the guests were from many different countries, cultures and languages. There were several Americans, many of them students, backpacking and camping like Tom was doing. There were only a few actual tents. Most of the folks had European RV's and some had the traditional VW camping van with sleeper and small kitchenette. There were also some pop-up trailers.

Finally, Tom was on a similar schedule as the other campers. When he went for his first morning shower, there were several other men and boys in the showers. It was amusing to see the American campers wearing bathing suits in the showers. Most of the Europeans seemed unfazed to walk around naked under the spraying water. Some of them even had their young sons with them, who were just as naked. Tom was observant. He noticed that when someone paid for hot water, the minute the one man finished, naked men rushed to the spot to take advantage of the free hot water for the duration of the purchased time. Tom laughed as he envisioned this exercise as an opportunistic orgy for hot water. Tom was shy. He dared to shower naked, but wrapped his towel

50

Liberating Tomas

around his waist while he finished shaving. He took notice that many other men stood stark naked as they shaved.

There was a beautiful central park downtown where groundkeepers were busy planting large fully bloomed blue hydrangeas. Tom had lunch at the Woolworth's cafeteria that Frommer's book recommended. Tom's curiosity led him to read the many posters stapled to the notices board. He realized that the next day a schedule posted for the installation of the governor of the castle. He felt fortunate to have accidentally managed to be in Edinburgh on the day when the people were going to celebrate. Tom felt privileged to witness all the pomp of the occasion.

That next day, it was unseasonably warm and Tom watched from wooden bleachers to see one of the kilted guardsmen, wearing the big Beefeater hat, faint in the heat. The bagpipes continued to play. It was an impressive display. The next day, he began hitching back to London. Soon after he first arrived in London, Tom bought a wool suit needing alterations. He needed to return to London in order to pick it up.

It was tough going south from Edinburgh. He traveled through Sunderland, Leeds, and then he was stuck in Sheffield. At the motorway rest stop, Tom sat near the door to the men's room so that he could benefit from the overhanging roof. He was tired and it was getting wet again. An old woman dressed in odd fashion walked by and saw him shivering.

"Well I'll be. You'll catch your death out here in the drizzle," she spoke directing her words at Tom. "I'm coming right back to get you. Wait just a few minutes and we'll get you a snack and a dry spot to drop off your stuff."

Tom wasn't sure if she was credible. He wondered if she was a little loony. .The woman returned shortly with a teapot of cold water and introduced herself. "I'm Gladys. What's your name?"

51

David Marty

"My name's Tom," he answered.

"Well Tom, you might as well come join my husband and me in our bus over there. You'll be a lot warmer and dryer."

Gladys wore a woven hat with dangling tassels. She appeared gypsy-like, probably in her sixties yet looking more worn than that. As they neared the old bus, she hollered to the open window, "Arthur, we've got some company."

Arthur opened the door to the bus and welcomed his wife and Tom. "Hello my lad. I'm Arthur and you are?"

"I'm Tom." He answered and Arthur put out his right hand to give a hearty firm handshake.

The new friends both had thinning white hair, but Arthur was also balding and wore a plaid jockey cap. Tom couldn't help but notice that each had misaligned and yellowed teeth. Arthur was even missing several teeth. He also sported a white mustache that seemed similar to the one on the Monopoly game piece man. They lived and traveled in an ancient modified school bus.

"Which direction are ye headed, lad?" Arthur asked.

"I'm trying to get back to London," Tom responded.

"That's a shame; we're headed the opposite way. We just drove up here from London."

Gladys heated water for tea and offered, "We have some biscuits and you should drink a hot cup of tea."

Tom thought that was an odd combination before he realized that biscuits in England were the same as candy bars back home. They served him tea and biscuits and were quite accommodating. Tom offered them some of his own cheese and bread. Gladys and Arthur lived a transient, on the road, bohemian life style. Tom could tell that they were not well off by any stretch of the imagination, but they were very hospitable and kind none-the-less. Tom felt comfortable in their company.

52

Gladys talked about many things. She asked Tom, "What is your sign?"

Tom answered, "I'm not sure what you mean."

"I'm sorry, I was wondering what your astrological sign is."

"I think I'm a cancer," he said. Tom knew little about astrology but was now interested in learning more about it. Arthur was often quiet and seemed to doze off frequently. Gladys busied herself trying to explain sun signs, moon signs. Her world of astrology was organized. Close to midnight, a car pulled into the rest stop with another, even older man and woman in it. Gladys excused herself and went out to talk to the pair. His sociable new friend returned to announce to Tom that she had arranged to have the older couple drive Tom all the way to London. Tom could hardly believe his fortune.

Devon and Claris were probably around seventy-five. They were on their way to London to meet a plane coming from Australia, which was to be carrying Claris' brother. She had not seen her brother in forty years. This couple was so cute and refreshingly candid. They were also certainly an answer to Tom's payers. Tom would never have had the courage to approach them in the rest area.

Claris was very excited to practice her Scottish accent on Tom. She looked at him carefully, and then spoke, asking, "Can you understand me?"

Tom smiled and encouraged her by replying, "Yes I understand you." After several other statements that she voiced, Tom reassured her, "Be sure to talk slowly and your brother will understand you too."

She continued to practice her speech all the way to London. They shared food and drink with him, which they had prepacked into a quaint picnic basket. Devon expertly drove the three of them. It took all night but they eventually arrived in London in the early morning. They arrived just before the congestion of rush hour traffic. Earl continued driving until they stopped at a relative's house in London where Tom became like one of the family. The hosts prepared a large English breakfast. After eating, the couple and Tom boarded the Tube. The couple was getting off at the airport connection. Tom was riding the subway further. When the Tube came to a stop at the airport exit, the woman folded some money into his hands and hugged him goodbye. It was about $5.00 US. She was so sweet!

Tom retrieved his suit, bought a pair of shoes, and dropped everything off at Molly's apartment because she was traveling to Minneapolis in a few weeks and she had agreed to take his things with her. Then he headed south to the freeway, which led to the English Channel Ferry. The second ride he got took him all the way to the ferry.

He ferried across the Channel in the late morning and arrived in France early afternoon. During the crossing, it occurred to Tom that the day marked his nineteenth birthday. How special it was to be crossing over to the continent on his birthday. Tom's plans included hitching along the Northern coast of France, into Belgium, Holland, through the northern tip of Germany, up to Denmark, and maybe even to Sweden.

He was excited to be on the continent. Now he had to pay undivided attention so that he could try to understand French. Tom was apprehensive about foreign speaking drivers but knew that he had to relax and take things as they come. *At least here, they drove on the right side of the road,* he thought.

One of the first drivers who stopped for him in Calais, France was a man in his mid-thirties. He was French and didn't speak a word of English. Therefore, the conversation was all in French, which Tom knew pretty well, but not fluently. Jacques had a small European truck and he strapped Tom's fifty-five pound Duluth pack onto the bed of it. He was heavy set and as the conversation developed, Tom soon realized that Jacques had a disability. His mentally challenged mind slowed his speech.

It was odd speaking French to a man who was challenged. Jacques started making some jokes that Tom didn't quite understand and then began pointing at the buttons on Tom's blue jeans. Soon Tom realized that he was interested in seeing his sexual equipment. After some time and a lot of prodding, Tom thought, *what harm would it be to show him?* He unbuttoned his jeans to show the man his penis. Jacques's reaction caught Tom off-guard. Jacques began to look at Tom with a somewhat crazed, ravenous gaze. More than once, Jacques' inattention to his driving nearly caused him to lose control of the truck. Most of his attention focused on Tom's crotch.

Jacques asked him, "Where are you planning to spend the night?"

Tom answered him, "I'm going camping in a tent at a campground. I have a sleeping bag in my pack."

To this Jacques responded, "I'll go camping with you and I want to make love to you."

Tom repeatedly said, "Non, non, non, I want to go camping alone!"

The standoff went back and forth for about a half-hour. While still conversing, they came to a little tavern and Jacques stopped the truck. They went inside and the Frenchman bought beers, one for each of them. Tom was hoping to run from him but his giant pack tied to Jacques' truck wasn't easily accessible; and Tom couldn't afford to leave it behind. They drank the beer from the bottles at the small bar inside.

David Marty

After the beers, Jacques began driving again and upon approaching a small shopping area, he told Tom, "I live near here and this is where I shop."

Knowing he was a little bit slow, Tom concocted a plan. He decided he'd relent and said to Jacques, "Okay, let's go camping together. It will be my pleasure to go camping with you."

Tom could see this delighted Jacques immensely.

Then, Tom followed up with this suggestion to him, "You need to change into more comfortable clothes for camping. Why don't you stop here and let me out. I can pick up something to eat from the shops right here."

Jacques let Tom out of the truck with his backpack and drove off to his apartment to change clothes. Tom agreed to meet Jacques in about a half-hour, right where he left him.

As soon as Jacques was out of sight, Tom nervously looked around to see where he could go or with whom he could get a ride in short order. The ride prospects didn't seem very good. Tom stepped into a small shop and purchased a baguette and some cheese, and a large bottle of Orangina to wash it down. Tom was scared that Jacques would come back and find him stranded there. He started walking as fast as he could in the opposite direction, his huge pack straddling his broad shoulders. About six or eight blocks away, he came upon some huge wind sculpted sand dunes, three or four in parallel rows, each about twenty feet high at their peaks and at least fifty yards in length. Tom walked between two of them and sat down. He was sure that no one from the road would be able to see him. Then he waited-- an interminable time--several hours. He hungrily ate the cheese and bread and drank from the bottle of orange soda. At one point, feeling safe, he even slept. When he woke up, he got out his pen and continued writing a letter home that he

56

started while onboard the ferry. He checked his map and decided he was near Dunkerque. By dusk, Tom was sure that the wild Frenchman would have given up all pursuit; and to his surprise, he found that he was within walking distance to a campground.

It occurred to Tom that Jacques could be waiting near the entrance to the camp but he entered the office and registered anyway. It was evening and the camp was near the shoreline. Tom's camping spot was on pure sand. The tent stakes wouldn't hold the tent down against the ferocious and constant winds. Tom had a fitful night as he put his heavy pack on one side of the tent, and his body on the other side, to weigh the floor of the tent down. He managed to get some sleep but not nearly as much as he had needed.

4   *Brussels Belgium 07-05-70*

---

4   © Borna/Dreamstime.com—Flower Carpet in Grand Place of Brussels Photo

David Marty

Dear Sis,

I've been in Brussels two days and have seen a puppet show and gone to my first dance. I met a girl from America who has been here four years. I missed the last streetcar so I had to walk to camp. Tell Mom not to worry. They have big meals here for less than $1.50. They also have good pastries. Hope you are having a good time at the lake. Did my younger brother buy his car yet? They speak both French and Flemish here and I had a free dinner on the way hitchhiking here. I'm heading for Amsterdam tomorrow. Hope I can get this in the mail soon. It's been raining or cloudy for about seven days now and it's supposed to be wet north of here too. It should get better weather when I start going south. I don't think I will be able to go to Sweden or Norway. Bye, Love, Tom

XIV

Belgium

The next morning Tom was out on the road again headed toward Belgium. He managed to get a lift from a nice looking thirty-something man who took him all the way to Ghent.

Frederick was anxious to show Tom pictures of his two young sons that he kept in his wallet. Frederick brought Tom to a restaurant and said to him, "Have anything you want on the menu."

"I'm not sure what some of this is," Tom said honestly.

"Let me order you something that will be hearty and nutritious then"

They both had a large lunch of fresh cooked whole flounder and salad. They ate together. It was the best food Tom had eaten in Europe, so far. Frederick was very friendly, gracious and generous. He was an executive and enjoyed telling Tom about the history of Belgium. Frederick paid the bill and left Tom as he continued on to a meeting. There never seemed to be any ulterior motives.

Tom was lucky and arrived in Brussels that same afternoon. He found the camp he was searching for and learned that he would have to take the tram to get to it. Once he registered for a campsite, Tom stocked up on food. His usual fare was yogurt, cheese, bread, fruit, and sometimes sardines. He learned to look for the bins of outdated food, which were highly discounted, often near the front door of the small food shops located at the camp entrance. Sometimes he would buy day-old bread, which was still quite fresh. Sometimes he'd choose oysters or even clams to take the place of sardines. He had to make sure to find cans with their own key opener included. He didn't have a can opener.

Tom found throughout Europe, most campgrounds played music on speakers set around the grounds and in the common buildings. The most popular song of the summer of 1970, *"Raindrops Keep Falling on My Head"* played frequently in most of the campgrounds. By the end of his trip, after hearing that song played in nearly every campground, its melody became one of those songs that you cannot get out of your head even though you desperately want to.

After raising his tent and buying a few provisions, Tom realized how exhausted he was. He removed his shoes and socks and looked at his swollen feet. There were large blisters on the outsides of both of his heels and one on his right big toe. He needed at least a day of rest before continuing. The weight of his pack was demanding too much from his feet. Tom felt instantly better when he was able to wander around without the big Duluth pack. He knew he'd have to spend at least one more day without hauling his home around with him. It also occurred to him that he wasn't gaining any ground by walking on when traffic failed to stop for him. The solution was going to have to be making signs for cities that were in the direction he wanted to go. Then he could sit and wait for just the right vehicle that was going his way. He'd observed other hitchhikers doing the same thing.

The second day, Tom decided to go to the center of the city. He knew the tram went there but didn't have a schedule. He began walking along the tracks, figuring he would just follow the tracks back at the end of the night. All the tracks came from outlying areas and converged onto the central square. After spending a long day watching a performance of a puppeteer, and standing on the sidelines of a dance for youth with rock music, eating some good street food, and watching the variety of people, Tom decided to go back to the campground. He missed the last tram out. Then he got confused as to which tracks to follow back. He chose the wrong ones and spent several hours, late at night, trying to locate the camp. It was nearly 2:00 in the morning before he finally reached the camp entrance.

The next morning, Tom was back on the road, made it to Antwerp in one ride. He waited a while before a young man stopped his car to offer Tom a ride. The driver introduced himself as Gerd and said he was in his early twenties. Tom felt an attraction to Gerd's dancing eyes. Tom gave him a warm welcoming smile. Gerd agreed to take Tom all the way to the border of Holland. As they talked, Tom discovered that Gerd's English was nearly flawless.

"I am in medical school here in Antwerp," he said with a smile. He was boyishly handsome with sandy short hair and dazzling blue eyes with a slight, yet muscular young build handsome face and cute, small ears. He seemed to be flirting with Tom. Tom enjoyed the attention and thought that Gerd was very handsome as well. He surprised Tom when they got near the border of Holland.

Gerd turned the car into a pasture and drove along a rutted dirt cow path. Then, he started leaning over to kiss Tom. He whispered to Tom, "Let's get more comfortable." He reached

David Marty

across Tom to recline the seat. Next, he moved over to the passenger side of the car. Gerd was kissing Tom deeply on the mouth, probing Tom's orifice with his wily tongue, while rubbing his crotch on Tom's clothed loins. Tom became alarmed when, from out of nowhere, a farmer appeared walking his cow which lightly brushed the passenger door where the two were thrashing.

Gerd said to Tom quietly, "Don't worry; it is a common thing for the farmer to see. People do this all the time here." Nevertheless, he used his own body to shield Tom from the farmer's glance.

After the farmer passed, the Belgian resumed his passionate kissing and heated body gymnastics. This kissing was all new to Tom. To have someone else's tongue in his mouth wrestling with his own tongue was such a novel experience. He noted the moisture, flavor, and texture probing his mouth and he pushed back with his own tongue. It excited Tom and he became aroused.

Tom could feel the sexual heat, which felt almost like embers inside of this delicious young man as he mounted Tom to thrust his pelvis into him. Tom was relishing the fact that he could get Gerd so worked up. Tom felt his own penis swelling from the excitement of the kissing and the friction of their loins. It touched Gerd's rock hard penis through their jeans jointly creating a rib of stimulating warmth. Gerd's heart began to race and his mounting rhythm became faster. The taste of his male hormones welled up and flavored both of their mouths. Then Gerd let out a big sigh and Tom realized he was having a stupendous, gushing orgasm. Both were fully clothed, but now Gerd's tan pants had turned dark brown over the entire front area of his crotch from the drenching wet and sticky semen. It was such an unexpected and thrilling experience for Tom to be a part of another man's orgasm in such close proximity, just by rubbing covered genitals. Tom marveled

62

Liberating Tomas

at the intense power of such a sexual encounter. It was immensely satisfying to Tom, even though he didn't erupt himself. Gerd collapsed in a heap on top of Tom.

It took a few minutes for Gerd to compose himself again. Then he casually resumed his driving position and, still in wet pants, drove Tom to the border guardhouse.

Gerd said very innocently, "It was a wonderful pleasure to meet you and I hope you have safe and eventful times on your journey. Thank you so much. I have to turn back now. Goodbye my dear friend." Tom got out of the car and Gerd circled the car around and drove off.

Tom decided that Gerd must be a homosexual but he didn't seem "perverted" to him. He admired the politeness and openness that Gerd possessed. Tom accepted that he was a willing enabler, but not necessarily a homosexual himself. Tom always remembered him for his scents and he felt privileged with Gerd's passionate sharing.

From the border of Holland, Tom continued toward Amsterdam. It was more difficult hitching here because the landscape was mostly either agricultural or wild grassland. He got a ride from a Danish family and sat in the back seat with their two young children. They didn't speak English so the bulk of the exchanges were in pantomime. Tom traveled with them through Breda and then to Rotterdam. Tom was surprised that parents of young children would stop for a hitchhiker who was a stranger. It would never happen in Minnesota.

The first ride from Rotterdam was from a van of European hippies. They seemed drugged already and there was a sweet smelling smoky haze in the van. The young woman offered Tom a pipe; she proceeded to light it after they were back to speed from picking him up.

63

Tom asked her, "What's in the pipe?"

She answered in English, but with a strong accent, "Hashish."

Tom was intimidated but decided that he should smoke a little bit just to be polite. It was his first time smoking anything, including cigarettes. He drew the smoke in and coughed violently. The woman smiled and demonstrated to Tom how to draw the smoke deep and hold it down in the lungs. He tried again but he didn't get much of a buzz because he wasn't yet adept at inhaling the smoke.

Windmill in Holland 07-10-70

Dear brother,

This is my second full day in Amsterdam. I saw some museums and Anne Frank's house. Today I also saw the flower auction. I'm going to the city this afternoon and take a boat

---

5 © NataliaBratslavsky/Dreamstime-Mill Photo

ride on the canals. It's been very hot but I don't know the exact temperature in degrees. They have flies and mosquitoes here but they aren't too bad. I really like camping over here and there are camps everywhere. I'm going to spend tomorrow here too and then go to Copenhagen. From the map it looks like it might take two days to get there but I hope it's only one. If you have a car, I hope you are enjoying it. Hope everyone and everything is fine back home. Everyone rides bicycles or scooters here.
Bye, Love, Tom

XV

Amsterdam

Tom got to Amsterdam toward evening and found the camp-ground he was looking for, located near the airport. The next morning, Tom went into town and found Anne Frank's house, which he explored, and then he stopped at several art museums. The city was busy with bicycles, which had their own raised lanes on which to travel. Cars were small, just like in most of Europe. A canal system wove through the city center and then spread into the countryside.

He enjoyed walking in the country near the campground and noted the simplicity and cohesion of the rural canals, which were sometimes used as transportation and other times used as moats to confine dairy cattle to pastures. Of course, there were massive fields of tulips. Tom bought some food supplies in Amsterdam. He was surprised at how bread dif-fered, ever so slightly but uniquely and distinctly, from one country to the next. Holland also had wonderful milk and cheese at low prices. Tom ate yogurt almost every day because his father had convinced him that replenishing natural bac-teria with local yogurt cultures would allow him to be able to drink the water without getting ill. This strategy worked throughout his travels. Apples were just coming into season and were always a welcome treat.

The next day, Tom went to the big flower market that was located next to the airport. There, fresh flowers were auctioned off and shipped by air to all parts of the world. When Tom arrived at the huge market, he wasn't sure which door to enter and wondered if there was a fee to tour. He tagged along with a French tour group and pretended to be a part of that group so he didn't pay anything for a look around. The flowers were beautiful. He'd never seen so many fresh-cut exotic blossoms in one setting. There were thousands. The mixture of fragrances was intoxicating.

In the late afternoon, Tom took a bus into Amsterdam and stopped at a small shop at the edge of a canal to look at the many local gifts that were on sale. The owner, who was a young man himself, seemed exceedingly friendly. He quickly approached Tom to ask, "Can I help you find something?"

Tom answered the congenial and handsome young man, "I'm only looking at the many things you have to offer."

The shopkeeper continued unabashed and said, "Take your time. The store is open until 8:00 in the evening. I will be finished then and perhaps I could interest you in dinner, my treat."

Tom explained to the friendly young man, "It would be much too late for me and I'd have trouble returning to the campgrounds."

The shopkeeper tried to prevail; "In that case, I can offer my home for you to stay overnight."

Impressed at the offer, Tom voiced, "Thank you for such a generous offer. I don't feel that I can accept it today."

Then Tom walked out the door as he felt the man's eyes staring him in the back. Tom couldn't help but wonder why people, especially young men, seemed so very friendly and welcoming in Europe!

Not far from the shop, Tom saw the glass tour boat docked. Earlier he decided to pay for a guided tour on the city canals. As he got ready to board the boat, a photographer snapped a photo of him. Tom went on the tour and at the conclusion, everyone filed off the boat and walked past a display with the developed photos for sale, which were hanging on a string at eye level. At first, Tom wasn't going to buy his, but thought again and noticed that the size was very similar to that of a postcard. He bought his photo and used it as a postcard to write home to his mom. His young sister, later in a letter, told him that Claire cried when she finally got the photo in the mail.

Liberating Tomas

Amsterdam 07-13-70

6   Reederij Plas Photo 1970

David Marty

Dear Sis,

Sorry again about the delay in writing. It took three days of travel to get to Copenhagen. I arrived at a camp late last night. By the way, this is a picture, which was taken just before going on a canal ride in Amsterdam. I thought you'd like it. It only cost about $.60. I had many good experiences on the road. I met one German family who invited me to stay with them when I go back to Hamburg. I also rode with two nice Danish families who didn't speak much English. I had to take a ferry from the peninsula to the island but I unknowingly sneaked on and didn't have to pay. I also rode with a Danish woman who picked me up along with two French boys. She only spoke French. I'll write later about Copenhagen and soon a long letter, which I'm working on. Only one rainy day since I last wrote. This is a new camp with modern facilities. They make their own bread daily and it's great. Hope you are having a nice summer. Love, Tom

XVI

Road to Copenhagen

Thomas had a few good nights of restful sleep. He continued to nurse his tender and blistered feet. On a Friday, Thomas decided to set out for Germany and Denmark. If all went well, he would even try to get to Sweden.

Not all went well. It took days to get through Germany and over to Denmark. It was a weekend with few cars on rural roads. On top of that, Thomas was unable to change his money. Therefore, he was unable to buy bread or cheese in the stores. He also had the wrong coins for vending machines. All he had in his pockets were a few guilders. Tom headed north and got a ride over the enormous dyke, the Afsluitdijk, which the Dutch built to wall off the Zuiderzee and reclaim land for agriculture. He traveled through Groningen, then on to Oldenburg and Hamburg, in Germany.

During one ride with a young German family, they offered him an apple. They also invited him to stay with them when he came back through Hamburg. That apple was all he had eaten in twenty-four hours. They were very nice and Thomas sat in the back with the two little girls. He had a soft and calming way with children. He finally was able to find a vending machine where his Dutch coins would work, although he spent three times as much as he would have using the proper coins. He was finally able to get something to eat.

Although he never felt hungry, he ate very little food for three days. On Sunday, he got rides that took him through Flensburg, Germany and Odense, Denmark. At one point, he shared a ride with two French hitchhikers. A little old Danish woman picked them all up in the rain. The conversation in the car was French, which everyone could speak. Thomas finally made it to Copenhagen late Sunday and found a campground not far from the center of the city.

By Monday, he was able to get back on schedule with his money and food. Thomas often augmented his typical road meals with milk, eggs, and fruit, (apples, oranges and plums). He boiled eggs in his camping tin filled with water. That made them portable and they could last a day or two. Tom was learning how important it was to plan when it came to currency changes in the different countries.

Tivoli 07-15-70

---
7 © Sepavo/Dreamstime.com-Tivoli Garden Photo

Dear all,

It's 5:00 AM here and the sun has been up for over an hour. I'm on my way to Munich, Germany in a Volkswagen. There are two of us and we hope to get to Munich tonight. Last night I visited Tivoli and it was just as beautiful as the picture. It's been cool and damp or rainy all the time here glad to be moving on to warmer weather. Can hardly believe that I won't have to spend money on train fare to Munich although I will help pay gas expenses. Will be writing from Germany soon.

Bye, Love, Tom

XVII

Copenhagen

Tom enjoyed Denmark. Part of the allure of this country for Tom was the fact that the purchase of pornography was legal and aboveground. Selling such material was punishable in Minnesota at the time. Tom visited a shop and paged through some magazines. He was especially satisfied there was a men's section with all male pornography. Tom was embarrassed to make a purchase and wasn't sure if he'd be able to take such materials back into the United States. However, he thoroughly enjoyed seeing eager men with proud erections in print.

Tom also took the time to explore a Modern Design Emporium. It featured beautiful glass and ceramic dishes and drink wear, sleek stainless steel eating utensils. Everything was well above Tom's budget. Off to the side of one display, imported wooden trivets from India were featured. Tom decided he could afford them and purchased three, sending them home by mail.

One evening he went to Tivoli Gardens. It was such a festive, yet dreamlike place. Many Danes, young and old, played in the long summer daylight. As nighttime approached, the amusement rides and walkways softly glowed with thousands of tiny party lights. He saw an outdoor ballet performance. It was the first time he'd ever seen a live ballet performance and loved seeing the men in their tight tights showing their well-developed rear ends. To Tom, the men seemed like beautiful strong stallions and the women seemed like feather-light fairy dolls.

There was a big university student hall in Copenhagen, which also served food in the cafeteria. Several times, Thomas ate there for very little money. Occasionally he would engage with other students if he heard them speaking English. However, he was still very shy, and often tended to observe and listen to people rather than dialogue with them. He spotted a bulletin board, which had postings for a variety of things. He checked the postings every time he was there and one day, he noticed a posting by a student who was driving all the way to Munich. The poster was looking for someone to share the ride and expenses. Tom decided to forgo Sweden, and most of Germany. He called the number on the post and accepted the offer of a ride with the student. They met very early in the morning, the sun was just brightening the sky and the birds were singing loudly even though it was only 3:00 AM!

It turned out the driver was an African named Desmond. His English was very good and the two shared many hours together. The conversation was comfortable. Desmond and Tom had many intellectual discussions about worldly issues. It was a long ride, but it more than made up for all the time that it would've taken to hitchhike that same distance. There didn't seem to be any hint of a sexual agenda, which Tom found rather refreshing. Tom paid for gas on one of the two stops they made. They got to Munich late that evening, and soon after, they parted ways.

Munich 7-20-70

Dear Sis,

    I had one very good day yesterday. It was the first time I've been hot in about six weeks. Today is rainy though. I was hoping to leave today but must wait until it's dryer. I just finished a really good dinner. Tomorrow, I think I'll go to Salzburg, Austria and camp in the Alps. I might go to Yugoslavia because several people have recommended it and they say no visa is required. Then I'll head to Italy-Rome, Florence, and Venice. You can write me in Rome. I met a guy from Tunis (Africa) and he and I spoke French for a few hours. He's going to Canada and I told him he could stay at our house if he was in the city. I hope there'll be no more rain after I cross the Alps. If there are more than one American Express Offices in Rome, I'll get to all of them so don't worry about that. Bye, Love, Tom

---

8 © Danbreckwoldt/Dreamstime.com-Munich in Germany Photo

XVIII

Munich

Munich was undergoing major construction in 1970 because the city was putting in a subway, preparing to host the Olympics. Before finding a campground, Tom met a middle-aged man who took a fancy to him. Bruno drove a Volkswagen and first offered Tom a ride into town. Bruno opened the front of the Volkswagen to put Tom's large pack inside. Then, he treated Tom to lunch and later to dinner. Tom was only beginning to learn that maybe men were so nice to him because they expected sexual favors in return. Being a virgin, Tom was not even sure how to perform such favors.

When they stopped for lunch, Bruno parked the car and Tom asked him, "How do you ever find your car again because it seems as if everyone drives the same white Volkswagen? They all look identical to me."

Bruno answered, "One has to remember where one parks. It isn't so hard."

Tom laughed aloud when, after lunch, Bruno tried to use his key to open the wrong Volkswagen. Bruno's face turned beet red from embarrassment.

David Marty

After a dinner of Knockwurst and Sauerkraut, Bruno tried to get Thomas to come to his home. He said, "I have a wonderful home in the suburbs. It is very remote."

Thomas soon discovered that Bruno's house was in the opposite direction of the campground where he wanted to stay. A remote house seemed frightening to Tom. How would he ever be able to get back to the camp if Bruno's anticipation suddenly soured?

Right away, Tom told Bruno, "I don't think I want to go that far."

Bruno advertised, "Several other American boys have been my guests and they enjoyed it very much."

Tom started getting nervous because Bruno was insisting that he ride with him to his country house. Tom had the strongest feeling that maybe Bruno was the kind of pervert of whom his parents had warned him. As Bruno got more insistent, Tom became more defiant. Then, very abruptly, Bruno started shouting at Tom in German, something unintelligible, and ordered him to get out of the car in the middle of a busy main street in Munich. He even stopped traffic to open the front hood and throw Tom's heavy backpack from his car. A startled Tom watched Bruno's abrupt change in demeanor. However, Tom was also glad to be free from him.

Tom thought about how it could have been his early demise. He wondered if the young American boys who enjoyed Bruno so much were still alive to talk about it. He wandered about, almost in a daze. Tom didn't want to cloud his journey with fear. He finally decided to go to the campground. Tom found the campground that was far away from the city. From the remote front gates, it required a walk, a bus and a tram to get back into the city. Tom took the trolley to the end of the line and waited for a bus. While he was waiting, a young man came up to him and started a conversation.

He had olive skin, spoke French, and told Tom, "My name is Mohammed." Mohammed was originally from Tunisia. They spoke to each other in French. He continued, "I'd like us to be friends. I'm very interested in Americans; in fact, I'am going to Canada in the fall and look forward to learning more about America. Where are you staying in Munich?"

Tom responded, "I'm staying at a campground. I'm on my way there right now."

He smiled and said, "I live near a campground with my grandmother!"

It turned out to be the same campground.

They talked for nearly an hour and exchanged addresses before the bus finally arrived. They both boarded and sat next to each other, continuing the conversation. Mohammed got off when Tom did and then they said goodbye. Tom walked toward the campground and Mohammed walked the opposite direction.

The next day, Tom decided he'd splurge and pay for a high-end restaurant dinner. Tom found his way into Munich and had a delicious hot dinner at a restaurant, dressed in his now quite shabby best clothes. He ordered the Sauerbraten. It felt strange to eat alone in a restaurant. He thought about the many days when he slept alone and met only fleeting strangers. After dinner, he tried to find a beer garden. He finally came across The Hoffbrauhus beer garden. Tom never even tasted beer before he got to Europe so he wasn't sure what to expect. He'd just turned nineteen and the drinking age at home was twenty-one. Bar maidens who could carry six in each hand served strong beer in one-liter glass mugs. Tom had two mugs of beer and prudently decided to cut himself off at that point. He was at a urinal when the man peeing next to him, an English person, asked him, "Hey bloke, why don't ya come and join my party?"

Tom was already tipsy and slurring his words while he attempted to say, "I think I've had quite enough already."

The older lad insisted and Tom, always wanting to please, acquiesced to the man. Tom followed the man back to the English party and had another mug of beer. Thomas wasn't sure if he had any more than that, but he soon decided it was definitely time for him to try to get back to camp. Thomas remembered stumbling onto the trolley. He was very drunk and awkwardly unsteady on his feet. The tram lurched to a stop and then started forward again. He had a vague recollection of vomiting on the trolley floor as everyone on the tram looked on. He was embarrassed. After that, he had a complete black out.

The thing he remembered next was waking up in the middle of the night because he had to pee. He was fully clothed, in his sleeping bag and in his own tent. Tom had a terrible headache and began to wonder how he'd gotten all the way to the campground. More alarming was wondering how he'd found his own tent out of all the others in camp and then got himself tucked into his sleeping bag without assistance. He thought of the possibility that Mohammed somehow assisted him in finding his tent. It would've been the best-case scenario. By morning, Tom became worried that someone else had found him and alerted the campground guards for help to get him to his tent. He had no memory of any of it, so he could only speculate. He felt so humiliated that he decided to leave the camp right away. Early in the morning, he set off toward Austria. It was horrible to wake up feeling sick and with amnesia.

Thomas best route was by way of the Autobahn where there were no speed limits. At first, he walked directly beside the freeway. Then two uniformed Nazi look-alikes with a big German Shepard dog approached him and made him get off the freeway and on to an entrance ramp.

They kept repeating, "Nichts an Die Autobahn."

Salzburg 07-23-70

Dear Sis,

I made it to Salzburg yesterday evening. Yesterday was sunny and warm and I saw the castle in the top of this card. This is the most beautiful area I've visited. The movie, Sound of Music was filmed in this area. Leaving for Yugoslavia today and hope to be there by tonight. Met some girls from the University of Minnesota

---

9 © Alexandr6868/Dreamstime.com-Salzburg Castle Photo

David Marty

who came over on another charter flight. Wish I had more time to see more of Austria and Switzerland. The camp here is located by the railway tracks and all night long, every ten minutes, big freight trains go rumbling by. I hope they don't expect me to pay an awful lot. I bet our niece has really grown. Have you been babysitting for her a lot? I won't have too many days in Italy but will take a train from Rome to where I will be working in France. Hope you are saving these cards! Love, Tom

XIX

Austria to Yugoslavia

Thomas was lucky and made it to Austria that evening with two rides. Salzburg was gorgeous. Tom toured the castle and felt as though he was in the movie, *"The Sound of Music,"* which was a new big hit then. He observed the shopkeepers, while paying attention to small details, such as clean sidewalk entrances and impeccably neat store interiors, they weren't compulsively neat like the Germans seemed to be. He only stayed a day-and-a-half and decided to travel on toward Italy. Thomas still had to get through the Alps and his hope was to try to make it to Trieste. Thomas was using handmade signs almost all the time now.

Thomas got a ride from an Englishman driving a small sports car with the steering wheel on the right hand side of the car--just like in England. Ned was driving so fast that Thomas became worried as they sailed through the Alps. Much of the time, he pretended to be asleep. He couldn't bear looking while Ned drove his car as if he was on a racecourse. The mountains had an awesome beauty with a feel of remote wilderness. The roads were full of hairpin turns and steep inclines.

While Ned was driving, he mentioned, "I'm going to Dubrovnik, Yugoslavia. You should consider going all the way with me."

Before leaving the states, Thomas read about some nude swimming and sunning areas near Dubrovnik; he was more than curious to go there himself. Thomas answered, "I'd love to go to Dubrovnik. However, America is in a cold war with communism (in 1970) and entering Yugoslavia would require me to have a visa."

The Englishman laughed and said, "I don't need a visa so you probably don't either."

Thomas told him, "I'm sure that I would be detained at the border until a visa could be issued if it were to be issued at all."

Sure enough, at the border, the border patrol detained Thomas and Ned took off, leaving him to fend for himself. However, he obtained a visa quickly. Then, Thomas tried to get another ride. Hitching in Yugoslavia wasn't easy. There were few cars, and of the few, most were very small. Unfortunately for Thomas, the packed cars didn't allow for even one more passenger. His first ride took him from Klagenfurt to Ljubljana. When Thomas finally got his second ride, on the outskirts of town, the driver told him it was against the law for a driver to stop for hitchhikers but the young occupants didn't care for that law. Thomas decided it would be too hard to travel by thumb all the way to Dubrovnik, so for plan B, he found a campground near Rijeka and settled in for some needed rest.

Almost immediately, he met a small group of college-age kids camping not far from his tent. There were two young men, Gerald and Gilbert from Great Britain, and a young woman, Celia from France. They hung out together having fun swimming, eating, and discussing world affairs. They readily welcomed Tom into their group. Tom was thrilled to have some companions.

One day, an overcast sky led the group to decide to visit the on-site tavern, where they drank beer, had snacks and engaged in heady and not so heady conversation. Tom was careful not to drink too much this time. The two English men hid many of their empty bottles behind a ragged, floor to ceiling curtain covering the only window. The bar maid, who wore combat boots and was probably in her sixties, worked all day, from 7 AM until 9 PM. Moreover, she worked the entire large room alone. At the end of her day, she counted the empties near their table and gave a final bill for the number she counted. Of course, the ones behind the curtains didn't make it into the total.

Celia had to return to her parents' tent. She left early. Gilbert was very much in the bag and needed assistance from Gerald and Tom to walk back to the small tent. Gerald invited Tom inside. They laid Gilbert out on the floor of the tent. It was warm in the tent so it made sense that Gerald would start undressing Gilbert. It didn't take long until Gilbert was lying naked; his entire front side visible. Tom became aroused when he saw the gorgeous young naked man.

Without skipping a beat, Gerald reached over and began to unbutton the fly on Tom's jeans. Then he slowly unbuckled Tom's belt to slide his pants off too. After two erections were exposed, Gerald deftly undressed himself and made it three. Tom removed his shirt and got even harder when it dawned on him that two other naked men were admiring him. Gerald began stroking Gilbert's beautiful uncut penis. Gilbert was barely coherent and put up no resistance. Tom watched, feeling his own penis expanding with anticipation.

David Marty

Gerald put his nimble fingers onto the head of Gilbert's shaft. He slowly stroked first the head and then the whole length down to his balls. Tom couldn't believe what he was witnessing. He thought, *"How could he be so bold as to pump his friend in front of me?"* However, Gerald seemed experienced; he must have performed on Gilbert before. Gilbert started to moan with pleasure. Tom decided he wanted a bird's eye view of the whole performance so he positioned his head to rest on Gilbert's firm abdomen. Now he was intimately close to Gilbert's throbbing shaft and Gerald's fingers. The view was stunning and much appreciated. After several minutes of Gerald's hand moving up and down on Gilbert, Gerald took Tom's hand and placed it on his own, which was firmly gripping Gilbert now moist, glistening, and self-lubricated penis. Gilbert gave an approving loud grunt. Gerald took his hand off the shaft and left Tom to continue pumping Gilbert with his hand. In Tom's hand, Gilbert's penis flared and grew to its maximum girth. Tom never held another man's throbbing penis before. A loud gasp from Gilbert signaled an imminent eruption. The impulses began and sperm continued to fly in huge streams. The white cream eventually splashed all over Tom's face and hair. It was breathtaking.

Gerald was only getting started. He motioned Tom to lie down on his back so that Gerald could mount him. Gerald placed his big penis between Tom's legs and began to pump his organ in and out of the makeshift orifice. Tom felt Gerald's warm meat bury into his naked thighs and then pull out in a cadence that seemed to be working toward a crescendo. At the same time, Gerald was licking Tom's face and devouring Gilbert's juices, which were now dripping from Tom's head. The excitement turned Tom on like never before. He couldn't have dreamt a better scenario. Tom gripped Gerald's smooth firm buttocks and used his hands to pull and push Gerald in and out of his thighs.

After sucking up most of the sperm that Gilbert had shot onto Tom's face, Gerald forced his tongue into Tom's mouth. Now Tom could taste Gilbert as well as Gerald's pheromones on his tongue. Tom was not even touching himself but he was so close to orgasm himself. Suddenly, Gerald let out a loud cry and pulled his thick shaft from Tom's loins. He shot load upon load all over Tom's shaft and balls. The heat of the warm sperm on Tom's penis caused him to release his own load, shooting his hot man juice everywhere.

Gerald collapsed onto the naked Tom and slithered on the slippery mixture of sweat and semen as all of the final impulses dampened. Gilbert sobered up enough to watch the spectacular finale. He suggested they grab towels and head to the camp showers. In the showers, they all admired each other's nakedness and afterglows and then began to rationalize that, after all, they were drunk, and boys will be boys. The intensity of the encounter never came up for discussion after that. Tom felt as if he'd reached yet another milestone. He also felt that this sex play was really only innocent sporting fun between horny teen boys. Tom's enjoyment by two horny strangers into such a fulfilling sexual frolic would stay with him forever. The shared sensuality was exquisitely exciting.

The next evening, all four, including Celia, dared each other to go skinny-dipping in the moonlight at midnight. It was a young and fanciful thing to do, but actually, somewhat creepy because there were no lighted trails and the Mediterranean water was dark and cold. The shoreline consisted of large rounded rocks and boulders, and Tom was afraid of sharks, jellyfish and octopi. Nevertheless, they all took a brief dip in the sea and shivered their way back to the tent site wrapped only in their towels, which they'd taken with them down to the sea.

For one meal at the restaurant in camp, Tom chose an affordable item from the menu. Even though the menu was in French, Slavic and Russian, Tom wasn't sure what he ordered, but when served, soon found out that he had ordered squid with all the little suction cups still attached on the tentacles. Tom ate it and it was ok, not his favorite but, it's all about the adventure.

Tom decided, after a couple days, that it was time for him to start heading toward Italy. He enjoyed the break from backpacking. He enjoyed his time with Gilbert, Gerald and Celia. Hitchhiking was challenging and often lonely. He often had more time than he wanted to meditate on his adventures. Tom was scheduled to work in southern France the end of July and it was already mid-July. He hitched to Trieste, Italy. Then, in one more ride, he made it all the way to Venice.

Liberating Tomas

10   *Sighs Bridge, Venice 07-29-70*

Dear everyone,
   I won't get to Rome until tomorrow some time. I spent two nights at a hostel in Venice and will now spend a second night camping here in Florence. I'm very anxious to hear from home. I hope you weren't upset about my going to Yugoslavia. It was the best country that I visited because it was clean, cheap, and the

---
10   © Gary718/Dreamstime.com-Bridge of Sighs in Venice Photo

David Marty

people were friendly and curious. It's very hot here. This camp is quite primitive compared to others I've been in but it has a good store and is close to the center of the city. There are many Americans in the camp. I hope I can find a good leather coat here and I'm thinking of sending my tent home. It doesn't rain often. I'm looking forward to my stay in France but it has come quickly. I've had some good luck on the road and hope it continues until Rome. I hope you're all having a good time at the lake and not having too many problems with Shadow.
Bye, Love Tom

XX

Venice

Venice was very romantic. The canals and the ferry busses were an interesting departure from regular traffic. Thomas stayed at a youth hostel in Venice because there weren't any campgrounds beyond the causeway that leads to the city. The history of Venice came to life and everywhere one looked, the intricate artistic details were stunning. Thomas walked through St Mark's Plaza and watched the pigeons flutter in all directions to avoid danger. One evening, he went window-shopping and saw the most gorgeous pair of shoes in a store window. Tom debated about the price, the ability to carry them along with all his other stuff, and went back and forth in his head about the purchase. Tom loved well-designed shoes. He finally thought he'd postpone the decision and he walked on. Half an hour later, Tom decided he really should buy what he liked; but he lost his bearings and became totally lost. He wasn't able to locate the same shoe store again.

After Venice, Thomas headed for the autostrasse and resumed hitching to Florence. He managed to get a good long ride from two young, attractive and flirtatious Italian women who drove a small sports car. They stopped at an autoplazza built over the freeway and they all had gelati and cappuccinos.

It was the first time that Tom tasted espresso coffee. The cups were so tiny but the flavor was so strong, even exotic. He used lots of sugar and cream.

In Florence, he stayed at a campground outside the city and was able to walk to town. The statue of David, as well as all the other artistry was utterly amazing. Thomas liked Florence more than Venice. It seemed more accessible and compact. The museums were incredible. The weather was hot and arid in July. The Ponto Vecchio was full of interesting but expensive shops. Thomas stayed a couple of days, had some good food, and rested up a bit. Then it was on to Rome.

Spanish Steps, Rome 8-02-70

I received both letters on the 31st and read them while sitting on these steps. I had to leave 11:00 AM on the first by train and am

---

11 © Sborisov/Dreamstime.com-Spanish Steps at morning in Rome Photo

Liberating Tomas

in Toulouse, France now. I take one more train and then a bus I think to get to work. I hope someone will know about it when I get nearer. I only had one day in Rome and didn't see very much. I can hardly imagine tornadoes over here when it rains there isn't much wind or lighting. I traveled by train along the Italian and French Riviera and saw the lights of Monaco last night. I met a few people on the train. I'm anxious to see what kind of work I will have to do and what kind of people will be there. I was surprised about brother's car. I bet it is very nice. I hope Shadow is not as "sick" as you seem to say.

Bye, Love, Tom

XXI

Rome

Rome was chaotic. Traffic was loud. Horns blared incessantly and no one seemed to follow directions. Thomas only had two nights and one full day in Rome. After establishing his claim at the campground, he strolled around the area to see the neighborhood. At twilight, he stumbled onto a parking lot at the foot of a large hill. He looked down at his feet and realized that the entire parking area was littered with used condoms. Thomas wondered why so many carelessly discarded condoms covered the asphalt in a Catholic country. What a terrible waste of sperm.

Tom again discovered the very primitive campground toilets that he first encountered in Yugoslavia. There was a hole in the cement floor and two raised footprints on which to step. One had to squat over the hole and hit the hole with one's effluents. This was the common toilet found in most southern European campgrounds

Earlier that day, he found the American Express office where he'd told his family they could write to him. He was surprised to pick up six large envelopes with multi-page letters tucked

Liberating Tomas

inside them. It was a warm sunny day. Thomas walked part way up the Spanish Steps and sat on the edge of them. He slowly opened each letter, starting with the chronologically first one. He laughed when he read Claire's warning to him not to drink the water. He'd written already saying he was drinking the local water. She wrote the same warning in the next three letters; each time she also warned him about creamy desserts and custards, which also spoiled easily.

Another amusing letter from Claire mentioned the trivets that Thomas purchased in Copenhagen. His mother wasn't sure what to call them but on two of the wooden trivets, one small round leg on each had broken off in the mail. Claire suggested that if he still had the receipt, he could go back to Copenhagen and have the shopkeeper "make it right." Thomas laughed because he realized his mother had no idea how long and difficult a journey that would be for two tiny feet of a trivet. He became aware that his family was never going to understand the size and dimensions of Europe.

With his time in Rome so limited, he planned on spending money to go on a bus tour of the Vatican. He signed on to the tour from the campground where he was staying. Thomas wasn't Catholic so he was unaware that there would be a dress code to enter the Vatican museum and the Sistine Chapel. The bus left the campground and drove directly to Vatican City. As the bus pulled into the big square, everyone got off and proceeded to the main entrance of St. Peter's. Just as Thomas was getting ready to enter, an official priest stopped him to say, "You are not allowed to enter wearing shorts." Thomas had nothing else with him to change into. Cast off to the side, his embarrassment escalated when he heard from the same priest, "You cannot sit on the

David Marty

steps to wait the two hours that your tour group will be inside."
The bus had already vanished.

There wasn't a bench or a seat of any kind. Thomas wandered aimlessly for two hours around St. Peter's Square and his animosity toward Catholicism just kept increasing. He'd wasted the money he'd spent on this excursion. There was no shade in the searing heat. He was hot, had no water, and had to keep walking. It was his worst experience in Europe to date. That afternoon, a dejected Thomas bought a third-class train ticket to Auch, France--just west of Toulouse. It was Tom's first ride on a European train. He boarded in the late morning the next day. The train went north out of Rome and traveled past Pisa, and up the West coast of Italy. Thomas only had a third class ticket, which didn't afford him any luxury.

When the train rolled into northwestern Italy, night descended. Evening came fast. Thomas tried to get a look at Monaco where the train stopped around midnight. He was unable to see very much of the city.

Up until Marseille, he'd managed to get a small seat on a bench inside a cabin on the train. However, at the Marseille stop, several school-aged children boarded the train. The conductor asked all able-bodied adults, especially men, to give up their seats. At two o'clock in the morning, Thomas found himself falling asleep while standing on a moving train grasping a stabilizer bar in the passageway. By morning, the train rolled into Toulouse where Thomas had to switch cars and move to a smaller train that continued on to Auch. He arrived in Auch around 10:00 AM.

12

Coliseum, Rome 08-03-70

Dear Sis, I found Lavardens and I'm now all set up to begin work. I had to walk the whole way from Auch. One doesn't have to work too hard here. The people who own the castle came Friday and talked about what they wanted done to the place. It might take most of August. We sleep in the lower floor of the castle but I probably will camp outside because it is so dusty inside. I can get mail here but the address is: There is a post office just down the hill. I am the only American here and everyone has been really helpful. I think I will learn French well.
Love, Tom

---

12 Postcard Photo

XXII

Road to Lavardens

Thomas disembarked and inquired of the railroad master the location and directions to the town of Lavardens. Then a stranger told him that the town was about fifteen kilometers down the small road leading from the station. There were neither buses, nor taxis. There wasn't much traffic either and Thomas ended up walking the entire way along a narrow blacktop road. As he walked, he thought about the yellow brick road from *"The Wizard of Oz."* There were few road markings. Thomas wondered if he would meet up with anyone interesting like the scarecrow, or the tin man. It seemed like a very long walk and it was rather hot with bright sunlight. Finally, Thomas followed the road up a hill. From the top, he looked down at the castle of Lavardens in the distance. It was an awesome sight. It perched on a rise in a valley. In the valley, surrounding the castle, were fields of giant sunflowers in full bloom. It really seemed as if he was entering Oz.

It took longer than he thought for him to get close enough to see the tiny village built around the castle. Thomas arrived around 2:00 PM and he was just in time for siesta. He approached the only café. It was quaint--there were baby ducks

Liberating Tomas

quacking and chickens running around loose. A small group of young people sat at cafe tables outside drinking Orangina. He went up to them and in his best French, explained to them, "My name is Thomas, the American, looking for Le Club des Jeunes l'Histoire." They responded, "We are the workers of the club, Sit down, join us, and after siesta we'll take you to our leader."

Thomas found it a bit humorous to see ducklings, cats, dogs and chickens mingling with patrons in the small cafe. Some of the youths even picked up baby fowl and allowed them to walk on the tables.

Thomas finally met the supervisor who was only a few years older than he was. The boss showed Thomas the site. He also showed Thomas where he was to sleep--on the sand floor of the castle. Then he explained the archeology project, which was a restoration of the town's seventeenth century castle. Later Thomas learned that a wealthy Belgian family bought the castle and wanted it to be a tourist stop for always-popular light and sound shows.

As Thomas was getting his bearings, a young man approached him. "Hello, I'm Patrick. I am English."

"Good to meet you Patrick, I'm Thomas from the United States."

There was an immediate attraction because language wasn't a barrier. Thomas and Patrick soon became best friends. Thomas suspected Patrick and he shared a physical attraction as well. Whenever possible, Patrick managed to be assigned to help Thomas in the archeological work. Patrick had a very slight build, which meant that the muscular Thomas did all the heavy lifting. Thomas felt Patrick watching. He sometimes put on a show of strength to impress him.

99

The living conditions were primitive. The only running water came from a spigot of cold water with an attached hose used to wash hands, dishes, and wheelbarrows, digging tools and for bathing. The toilets were a grouping of out-houses built of stone that were used by most of the town. Food was mostly bread with yogurt, cheese, and occasionally some meat--like ham. Coffee with milk served in a large soup bowl was the offering in the morning. Usually there was soup or stew for lunch. In addition, there were always baguettes of French bread.

There were about twenty young adults from fifteen to twenty years old. The life in the club was communal. The entire crew rotated jobs of sweeping the "dining room", washing dishes, cooking, clearing tables. Often they would wipe the tables with pieces of bread and then throw the bread on the floor where the dogs would compete for it. It wasn't terribly sanitary and before long, two of the three English kids got sick.

The boys slept in a separate room from the girls. Sand fleas infested the whole place and because the floors of the old castle were thick with sand, and with young blood to feed on, those fleas were thriving. Once the volunteers climbed into their sleeping bags, they could feel the little bugs crawling, biting, and feeding on them. They would wake with ugly red welts on their arms and legs. Thomas tried to keep himself clean so that the fleas would find someone dirtier to suck.

The work was hard and grueling, yet the pace was their own. They moved piles of stone and dirt with pickaxe and wheelbarrows. During siestas, they sat under shade trees. It was the hottest time of the year and the sun was sweltering at midday. Several of the workers would hang out under the nearby plum tree to eat as many plums as they could pick. It was also during this time that Thomas discovered tobacco. Many of the other kids, for lack of anything better to do, would buy Gauloises cigarettes--Turkish tobacco with no filters. They inhaled the smoke deeply to get lightheaded and dizzy. Thomas learned to get high from smoking and enjoyed smoking after the midday snack, usually warm fresh French bread with a generous piece of chocolate.

There was an old pump organ in the church at Lavardens. Thomas discovered the organ one day and since he'd taken several years of organ lessons, his new friends asked him to sit down and play. He only played once because he didn't want to offend the church people. He was only able to play popular music by memory. Fully immersed in the French language and culture, Thomas felt at home.

13

Lavardens 8-12-70

---

13 postcard photo (1928)

David Marty

Dear Sis,

I expected a letter from you Monday and that's when it arrived. You sound as if you are having a wonderful time. I'm really enjoying it here. It rained three days and they had tornadoes--the first in the history of this part of France I think--down south of here. It's hot again now though. I haven't been doing hard work and I've been eating a lot so I am probably getting fat. The village kids keep coming around to talk to me because they like to hear my accent. We've had a few parties and campfires, which are fun. It seems hard to believe that I've already been here one and a half weeks. Love, Thomas

XXIII

Southern France

Near the end of two weeks, workers installed bleachers and lighting for the inauguration of a sound and light show. An historical script written about the castle and parts of the castle were to be on display. The workers were supposed to dress as if they were from the 17th century. Of course, none of them had period outfits, so they did their best by improvising.

Before all this took place, some of the group organized a little party. They made a fire in one of the castle's fireplaces. That morning, Thomas noticed that his camera was missing. He carried his camera all over Europe, often hesitating to take pictures because the moment never seemed right. He preferred to live his trip rather than take time to record it. Instead, he purchased postcards of things he wanted to remember. He was sure someone had stolen his camera. He asked his closest friends. None of them knew or heard anything.

The next day, after the fire burned out, Thomas was cleaning out the fireplace when he discovered his camera, destroyed by flames. Someone had hidden it in the fireplace not knowing that a fire would damage it that evening. He reported it to the female owner of the castle. She sent Thomas with her husband to the gendarmerie where a gendarme interrogated him. Thomas suspected that the two Italian kids had stolen his camera. They were suspiciously missing the day after and had abruptly left the group to go back home to Italy.

Postcard, Abbey at Moirax

Dear All,

Sat. we received word that the work at Lavardens was nearly finished and today, Sunday, we were all transferred here to Moirax. There's an eleventh century abbey here and we have to dig trenches on one side of it. It's much cleaner here, there are more people in the village, but it's not quite as charming. There are now only twelve of us for work as the others have finished

---

14 Postcard Photo (1947)

their term of work. They will be forwarding my mail sent to the old address and the new one is... Tell me how older brother made out with university registration etc. and about working at the market this fall. Love, Tom

XXIV

Moirax

The next day following the first light and sound show at the castle, the remaining kids from the Le Club des Jeunes de l'Histoire, who now numbered only eight, transferred to Moirax, another small village. In soft whispers, those in charge told workers that the flea situation had worsened and their health was now in serious jeopardy. Therefore, they transferred everyone to work on an eleventh century abbey. Rainwater was draining from the roof of the church and seeping into the stone foundation. The project consisted of digging a drainage ditch from the outside base of the church to a well in the middle of a grassy courtyard. The depth was to be one meter deep.

This time, the sleeping quarters for the boys was in an open-air roofed stable. The girls slept on the first floor of the old courthouse. The gnawing sounds of rats woke the girls each night as the rodents feasted on the cantaloupe set out to ripen in the windows. Before very long, everyone slept in the stable. This town was also very small--maybe forty-five people. All the indigenous villagers told Thomas that he was the first American they'd seen since WWII. They worked hard and toward the end of his stay--which was going to be another two weeks, Thomas'

106

pick hit a stone sarcophagus. The instructions were, tell no one, as it would be disturbing the peace of the dead. In addition, a reporter from a newspaper out of Agen, France came to do a story on the group. He interviewed all of them. Then he wrote a full-page article in the local newspaper. He even wrote about Thomas being from Minnesota (near the border of Canada was the best that Thomas could explain it). Thomas was quoted by the reporter, "The digging was familiar to me because the yards back home were very large; and I am used to working in them."

Next to the abbey were living quarters of a local family. They weren't in residence at the start of the work but showed up later. All of the kids were amazed to see the license plates on the car that showed that the car was registered in The Canary Islands. The ancient village was home to a handful of older men who spent their afternoons playing boules, seeing who could throw their large metal balls closest to a small target ball. The playing field had only two big lone oak trees on either side of the field offering little shade from the hot summer sun.

In Moirax, cornfields surrounded Thomas, not the sunflowers of Lavardens. Being a Midwest American boy in August, Thomas was craving sweet corn-on-the-cob. When it came to his turn of cooking, he asked if he could make corn-on-the-cob as a vegetable. People looked at him as if he had suggested some absurdity. In France, farmers grew corn for animal feed used with geese and pigs. French people never ate corn. Furthermore, the corn growing around him was field corn--not sweet corn. However, Thomas was determined.

He went to the grocery store and asked the storeowner using his French, "Can you get me some ears of corn?"

There were some communication problems because she asked, "Do you want mature corn?"

David Marty

He answered, "Oui".

The next day, she had about twenty ears of dried corn from last year's crop.

Thomas protested his disappointment by explaining, "I needed the kernels to be soft."

She apologized and in French, she informed him, "I can't get corn like that for you."

Then Thomas took his friend, Patrick, went directly to a farmhouse, and talked to the farmer. The man who answered the knock on the door was the most beautifully sensual man that Thomas had ever seen. He was thin but muscular. He had long-ish blond hair with a soft wave, which tossed lightly in the breeze. His blue eyes were crisp and Thomas was immediately smitten.

After blurting out his request to the man, the farmer repeated to Thomas what everyone had already said, "My corn is not for people."

Thomas said, "I would still like some so that I can cook it for my group."

Then he looked at both of them and relented, "You may pick some right from the stalks but please be careful not to damage the field."

Thomas and Patrick picked about twenty ears and took them back to the kitchen. Thomas found a big kettle. Then he filled it with water and put sugar and salt in the water, boiled it, and threw the shucked corn into the pot to cook for fifteen minutes. It wasn't quite as sweet as back home but the kernels were still young and it was close to what he had wished. Some of the kids thought the corn was good. One girl from Paris decided to bring corn home to her family when she left. Others thought it seemed heavy and hard to digest.

The funny thing was that the next day, all the women of the village stopped Thomas to ask him for the recipe for the corn.

108

Liberating Tomas

They'd all heard the rumors and wanted to try it for themselves. Thomas felt at home in this sleepy French village. He gave rides to the young children with his wheelbarrow. There was a big house in the village that had a huge cement pond built for washing clothes. Thomas and the others splashed in the cool waters during siesta and it served for bathing as well.

15

Dear Sis,

I received your letter about the water skiing. That's great! We are sending you a thank you in French for the great bars but one of the guys put it in the mailbox with only thirty

---

15 Moirax, France, inside the abbey 08-28-70

francs for a stamp so I don't know if you'll get it. There are only six of us now and we all leave the 31st when I will start hitching again with Pat. I doubt if I'll get to Morocco because I only have twelve more days before Paris. I was in the paper today and they even printed a quotation from me. I hope you like school and your teachers. Love, Tom

Dear Sis,

Well, I leave here tomorrow morning and will go as far as San Sebastian, Spain with Pat and a friend we met here. I will be sad to leave here. I got letters from the two older sisters! I

---

16 Photo 1970

Liberating Tomas

expect to spend eight or nine days in Spain and three or four in Portugal, and the rest in Paris. I'll be sending a long letter soon but I don't know when I'll be able to stop at a post office. I am fine—haven't been sick yet. I've been eating lots of fresh fruits and vegetables. See you in about twenty days.   Love, Tom

XXV

On to Iberia

Time sped by and soon it was time for Thomas to leave. Thomas wanted to go to Barcelona next. Two others from the group were heading to Spain. They offered to give him a lift to the border. Patrick pleaded to travel with Thomas, at least into Spain, until he needed to return to England. In the meantime, Danny, a French boy, desperately wanted to buy his canvas pup tent. Thomas didn't want to part with it but eventually Danny offered more than twice what he'd originally paid for it. Selling it would significantly lighten the load of his backpack. Thomas expected Spain and Portugal would be dry in late August, so he allowed Danny to buy his memorable tent.

When it was finally time to leave, the two French, the Englishman Pat, and Thomas got into a basic old Citroen and drove off toward Spain. Very early on, it occurred to Thomas that they seemed headed west instead of east to Barcelona. When he finally asked the driver, the driver responded, I'm driving to Biarritz, France on the border of Spain." Thomas checked his map and decided that he and Patrick could hitchhike east through northern Spain to Barcelona. The current ride lasted a few hours.

Biarritz was a resort town and active at the time because most of the French took nearly the whole month of August for holiday. Pat and Thomas left the two French boys and started to hitch a ride to San Sebastian, Spain. It only took one ride to get to San Sebastian. Then, according to the map, they needed to head to Pamplona. Thomas once read about the running of the bulls there. It was in a Hemmingway novel but he wasn't sure what time of year that took place. The two made it to Pamplona and discovered that the bulls just ran the previous week. Now the town was sleepy again. Pat and Thomas sat at a café and sipped on a beer. Then they resumed hitching on the east side of Pamplona. Nevertheless, they were in Basque country and in mountains. Pat and Thomas tried desperately to hitchhike toward Barcelona. It seemed hopeless so at dusk, they settled down to spend a night in a field just east of town in sleeping bags.

17

Bilbao, Spain 09-03-70

---

17 © Borjalaria/Dreamstime.com-Cathedral of Santiago, Bilbao Photo

113

Dear brother,

I'm still at the private beach camping but will probably leave tomorrow. This morning, Pat left for Paris and then back to England. I bought a leather jacket yesterday. It wasn't on sale but I only paid about $50.00 and I got it at a good quality store. I think I'll start tomorrow to get to Portugal in as little time as possible. Hitching is really bad here but I left most of my things in a locker at a train station. I'll have to pick them up when I come back to head for Paris. It's cloudy here now but still warm. Things are quite cheap here too—especially the food. See you in two-and-a-half weeks.   Love, Tom

XXVI

Welcome to Spain

They were at the same spot on the road one entire hot day trying to go further east. Not one car stopped. Eventually, Thomas decided they should go back toward Bilbao. They eventually got a ride with two women who just happened to be identical twins. Shortly after climbing into a car near Bilbao, the police stopped the car they were riding in. It was the '70s, during the late Franco period and rules forbade hitchhiking. As the driver stopped, one twin turned to Thomas and Pat from the front seat and explained that the driver didn't have her papers so she would give the police her own papers. As the police were talking in Spanish to the driver, her sister was talking to Thomas and Pat in English. She told the boys how both sisters loathed the police and how they hated the fascists

Soon after, Pat and Thomas found a place near the sea that was an open field and decided to set up camp there. Thomas spent only two nights. It was the first time that Pat and Thomas could finally relax in a bit of privacy. They were on the coast, only fifty yards from the ocean, which they could hear crashing against the steep cliffs. They both had something to eat and shared some stories with each other.

They decided to go to sleep just as nightfall approached. Each had a sleeping bag. Thomas was almost asleep when Patrick woke him and asked if he could share his sleeping bag because he was cold. Thomas could see why he was so cold—he was stark naked. A smile broke out on Thomas' face and he sprang out of the bag, undressed completely and offered to share his sleeping bag with Patrick. Pat brought his own sleeping bag over and they used Thomas' bag for the bottom and Pat's for the top. They slipped between them and began to cuddle with each other to get raise their body temperatures.

Thomas always thought that Patrick was interested in him but hadn't encouraged him because Pat, who was slightly younger than Thomas, had a smaller, boyish body. The two of them wrapped themselves around each other. This in turn played on Thomas' emotions and led to an arousal of large proportions. Thomas clutched Pat tighter and felt the transfer of body heat between the two of them. He began to kiss Pat's mouth sweetly. Pat rewarded Thomas by opening his mouth so that their tongues touched.

Patrick started to whimper because this was his first time with a man and he'd been hoping that his first time would be with Thomas. Two sets of hands began to explore the bodies not attached to them. Thomas relished the young, firm, tight body of Pat. Pat marveled at the lean, muscular man that he was finally able to hold and touch. In anticipation, both had erections with precum oozing. Thomas got the bright idea that he wanted to taste the slippery fluids coming out of Pat's penis so he moved his head lower and contacted the swollen shaft with his mouth. The reward was a sweet, indescribable and private taste. Thomas continued to feed on the penis, encouraging Pat to explode.

Patrick never felt anything like this before and thought he'd died and gone to heaven. He wanted this wonderful sensation to last forever but instead, he shot his load down the throat of Thomas. The semen gushed into his mouth catching Thomas unprepared. Fluids forced themselves to the back of his throat, and then flooded into his nostrils and at the same time, down his throat. Pat gave him the most personal and primal part of him. Thomas was overwhelmed. Thomas' penis was dripping wet with all the sexual excitement and he only had to rub it on Pat's now deflating shaft to deposit his own load on Pat's penis and scrotum. He fell back in pleasure. Instead of immediately falling asleep, Thomas pondered the joy and exhilaration of loving another man and marveled at the tenderness that the two had so willingly shared.

After that first night at the ocean, Patrick left to go back to England. Thomas thought about how he'd been a role model for Patrick and hoped that he was able to positively influence his co-worker. If only he could find a role model himself! He was saddened to see Patrick leave.

The second night, Thomas was alone. By early morning around 4:00 AM, it started to rain. At first, it was just a light drizzle and he managed to stay dry. However, after about an hour, the rain was coming down harder and the temperature was dropping. He thought about going to the nearby restaurant attached to a house but there was a large watchdog, it was 3 AM, and the lights were unlit. He wasn't sure what to say to a guard dog that only responded to Spanish, when he only spoke French.

In the rain, he got up and paced the ground to try to keep warm. He was miserable. By sun up, Thomas was thoroughly drenched and had premonitions of catching pneumonia. As the sun rose, the clouds appeared as if they might be breaking up.

David Marty

Then an hour later, more rain. He finally rolled up his water-logged stuff, which now weighed more than three times what it used to. He got a ride from a young truck driver inland over the northern mountains to Vitoria. He'd unloaded some of his things in a locker in Bilbao aiming to return on his way back to Paris to pick them up. He also bought a leather coat in Bilbao and left it in storage as well.

Once he got to Vitoria, the sun was shining and it was getting hot. Thomas spread his wet sleeping bag on the ground to dry and rested for a couple of hours. His stuff was not totally dried but he was getting inquisitive stares by people passing by, so eventually he resumed his journeys. Hitchhiking in Spain was more challenging than he'd ever imagined. Thomas knew little about the country. He didn't speak the language. Franco was still alive but with ineffective power. Tom remembered traveling through a cork forest and was surprised when he could smell the same aroma of the cork bulletin boards at home. The cork was bark from a type of oak tree, shaved off for harvest. Apparently, it could re-grow and be harvested repeatedly.

Thomas took a ride for as long as a driver was going his way; then by nightfall, he walked off the road from where he quit the ride. He'd find a spot that seemed safe and secure in a field, roll out his sleeping bag. Finally, he'd fall asleep in the dark. He would be sound asleep within five minutes, and then up at dawn. In the blackness of night, he wasn't always able to scout out his sleeping area with any thoroughness and sometimes woke up to unusual circumstances.

One morning he woke up to find he'd spent the night on the edge of a huge garbage landfill. After waking, he wondered if rats crawled over him during the night. Another time, he woke at dawn. Not twenty yards away, was a donkey and his master

118

Liberating Tomas

collecting pinesap from pine trees around him--Thomas thought maybe to make turpentine. Another evening, he was unsure of what was happening, but it seemed as if fireworks were exploding in the air nearby almost all night long. Thomas was never certain if it was some sort of night festival or if he was camped on the edge of an artillery range.

In Western Spain, four Americans in a van stopped to pick up Thomas. One of the women rolled down the window and asked, "Hey, Where are you headed?"

He was surprised that it was so easy to talk and listen to his native language again. "I'm going to Portugal, eventually Lisbon," Thomas replied.

"Hop in, we're going to Fatima but we'll be camping in Northern Portugal tonight."

As Thomas rode along with them, they talked about many things, mostly about their recent travel adventures. Two were male medical students on break and the other two were their girlfriends. As they got closer to Portugal, the countryside began to transform itself, looking bleaker and poorer than anything he'd ever seen in Europe before.

When the van pulled up to the entrance of the first campground just inside the border of Portugal, Thomas saw desperate beggars dressed in rags. They were so skinny; he could see the outlines of their skeletons. Five emaciated people, whose sex was indistinguishable, stood flailing their arms hoping for any sort of handout. It was as if they were zombies. They were almost blocking the road near the camp entrance that the Americans decided to stay at for a night. It was heart breaking. The campground had fences of chain link twelve-feet high with razor wire on top. It looked like a fortress, but Thomas was thankful

119

David Marty

because it would've been dangerous to be sleeping in a sleeping bag outside the fence.

Thomas judged the Americans of being overly cautious. They wouldn't drink water except purchased bottled water. They dipped all the fresh fruit in a chlorine solution before eating it. They were constantly washing their hands, food, and dishes with disinfectants. Thomas had long ago decided that he would drink water, use ice cubes, and let yogurt do battles with his intestinal flora. It seemed to have worked fine so far.

The next day they reached Coimbra, and drove on to Fatima. Our Lady of Fatima had appeared to three children several years ago and now there was a huge shrine commemorating the site. At Fatima, Thomas toured the big Cathedral and looked at all the crutches and wheel chairs hanging from the walls, from those assumed to have been healed by the shrine. The Americans he rode with were going to stay there longer and Thomas was anxious to get to Lisbon so he left them and began hitching south. None of the small cars stopped, but thankfully, he didn't encounter any more begging.

* * *

Marco was driving back from a visit to his sister's home in Porto. He was feeling good about himself and was driving fast from self-adulation. The time he spent with his sister was always good, but this time, she picked at a scab in his life. Her words haunted him as he drove even faster.

Teresa had confronted him and said, "Marco, you have everything going for you in your life now. You've become a vice president of Holiday Inn, Portugal. You have a beautiful apartment in Lisbon and more wealth than you can possibly spend. I also know

120

you can be generous and you have a big heart. Nevertheless, I worry for you because you are still single and have no one to share your successful life. I know it may be more difficult because you're gay, but I think you'd be much happier if you found someone to share your life." His mother had recently told him the same thing.

Marco's father, Werner, moved to Lisbon in 1939 when he fled Nazi Germany to seek refuge in Portugal. He finished medical school just before he left Germany. He married Angela a year later. Marco was born in October 1943, before the end of World War II. Angela had an uneventful home birth, customary for the times in Portugal. Werner and a midwife delivered the little bouncy boy.

Marco grew up in Lisbon in a happy, nurturing family. He had a sister, Teresa, who was two years younger than he was. Werner was educated and principled. Angela was loving and respectful of her husband and children. A traditional mother, she readily sacrificed her own needs for those of her children. From early on, Marco began to assume a role of caretaker.

Portugal didn't have its first television station until 1957. Radio was more the staple in people's homes. In Portugal, role models and character influences for youth growing up were mainly the people that had direct contact with them. Marco admired and mimicked his father. His set of morals were a combination of his mother's independent Portuguese heritage and his father's strict adherence to justice. With an historic Portuguese influence, Marco had other role models of courageous explorers, educated royalty and religious figures. Marco's maternal grandmother, Luisa, lived outside of Lisbon near the sea. Marco loved to go there and frolic in the wider

David Marty

spaces. Marco could remember chasing chickens and plucking eggs from their nests as a boy.

In Lisbon, but even more so in the country, people often led semi-communal lives. Mostly extended family but also friends looked after each other. Country gardens were large and tended by several different families. The elderly most often lived in the same family home that held up to three generations. Even in Lisbon, friends and family united to maximize the impact that they could have on their living standards. Neighborhoods were close-knit units of familiarity.

Marco enrolled in Catholic school where nuns and clerics taught uniformed boys and girls separately. He was a good student and excelled in his classes. He was also good at soccer. He especially enjoyed the camaraderie of his fellow teammates and loved to play around in the group showers. Often, he'd deliberately drop a bar of soap so that he could flash his pretty rear-end to his naked friends.

Marco always rushed to get home from school to see if he could help his mother. Marco didn't buy the century's old division of labor that still was popular in Portugal. He felt that the current dictator, Salazar, had institutionalized woman slavery. Women seemed burdened with all the mundane chores of daily living, while men went off to work, if there was work. Salazar's social policy was definitely gender biased.

Marco was lost in thought as he approached Fatima, where he had to take a turn onto a different highway. He slowed down and happened to look toward the shoulder of the road when he saw what he could only describe as a Greek God standing alongside the road with his thumb up, looking for a ride. The young man had perfect posture, broad shoulders, and muscular

Liberating Tomas

yet slim physic. Wearing cut off shorts, Marco saw the beautiful athletic legs. He stood next to a huge backpack holding a sign that read "Lisboa." The unflawed youth immediately captured Marco's heart. He pulled off the road just beyond the hitchhiker and looked back to nod, letting the beautiful young man know he had a ride.

Thomas hopped into the sports car and introduced himself. "Hello, my name is Thomas, I'm American." he said. He was finally getting comfortable meeting strangers.

Marco reciprocated by saying, "Very nice to meet you Thomas. My name is Marco."

Both men began to size up one another. Thomas thought that Marco might be about twenty-eight. He was driving a very pricey Fiat convertible sports car and spoke English with a British accent. The man was very handsome with freshly barbered thick wavy blond hair, dark brown eyes, and a classical chiseled nose and forehead. Marco appeared very prosperous by Portuguese standards. He was dressed in white linen pants and a playfully tailored shirt that outlined a muscular physic. Thomas also noted the expensive Italian shoes that Marco was wearing. Thomas had to inquire because Marco appeared Roman. "So, you are Portuguese?"

Marco replied, "Yes, I am. We are a culture of many diversities." He tried to hide the obvious fact that this young man was tunneling straight into his heart. He registered Thomas' gentle face and beautiful brown cow eyes, his longish wispy sun bleached hair, and his honest naïveté that suggested a certain vulnerability. He seemed very refreshing for an American. Thomas got the impression that Marco felt as if he had died and gone to heaven.

Alfama, Portugal 09-08-70

Dear Sis,

Well I got here although it took three-and-a-half days from Bilbao. I'm staying in a camp in Lisbon, which has a swimming pool, and in two hours, I'll be going to a camp on the ocean. My last driver was going there today and offered to take me. Tomorrow I head back to Bilbao via Madrid and then Paris. I've spent a few nights now sleeping in the fields but I prefer the camps. This card shows one of the areas of Lisbon although the main city is much more beautiful and clean. The only dolls they have here are plastic so I'll probably buy one in Paris where they should have everything! See you in about a week. Love, Tom

---

18 © Chrisdodutch/Dreamstime.com-Old House in Alfama in Lisbon Portugal Photo

XXVII

Lisbon

As they continued on the road to Lisbon, Marco told Thomas that he lived in Lisbon and knew of the campground where he was planning to stay. Marco offered to take him to a better campground where he could view the ocean. Thomas accepted this offer. As they got closer to Lisbon, the beautiful flowers that lined the freeway on either side and in the median impressed Thomas. There were thousands of brightly colored bougainvillea climbing the retaining walls with fragrant Oleanders clustered in rows. Closer to the center city, there were some flowering Birds of Paradise in bloom. Varieties of palm trees and tropical ferns framed flowers with their green lace. The floral perfume wafted through the air and seemed to cancel out the pollutants of truck and car exhaust. Lisbon seemed to be a rich mixture of ancient and new buildings and colorful tropical foliage. Marco drove Thomas right up to the front gates of the campground. As Thomas was leaving the car, Marco asked him, "What are your plans for tomorrow?"

Thomas didn't even hesitate. He replied, "I'm on holiday and I have no plans for tomorrow yet."

David Marty

Marco offered, "Let me pick you up at this same spot, outside the camp gate, around 9:30. I have tomorrow off and I would like it very much if I could show you Portugal."

It was an offer too good to be true. Thomas eagerly answered, "Yes, I'll be here."

Marco smiled with giddiness as he pulled away from the gates and drove off to his house in Lisbon. Thomas relished the idea of escorting such a beautiful and educated Portuguese man on a full day's adventure. He'd been looking for a masculine role model who was also kind and gentle. Thomas suspected he might be gay.

Thomas settled himself in the camp, but was uncomfortable there. No one spoke English or French. He didn't know a word of Portuguese. However, he got a good night's sleep. Thomas dreamt about the handsome and sexy Marco and the day ahead.

Bright eyed, showered, and dressed as neatly as possible with his limited wardrobe Thomas was ready even before the designated time. His handsome driver arrived punctually. Marco first drove Thomas around Lisbon and pointed out his house--a large townhouse perched on a steep hill overlooking the Tagus River. They went to some shops where Thomas found a lovely pewter lamp that looked like it was an antique but was actually a modern reproduction. He bought it and Marco helped him take it to the post office to ship to his mom back home. Confusion arose over shipping the lamp. The only packing material available was straw, unsuitable for overseas packages. Newspapers were the only things they could offer as packing.

The two went to have a late breakfast at a restaurant. Thomas was surprised that Marco ordered a bottle of wine with the meal. After the meal, they drove along the

126

Liberating Tomas

river going north from the city. Marco showed Thomas the Portugal that only a long time native would know about. They also drove to Cabo da Roca, the point furthest west on the continent of Europe. Later, Marco continued to nearby Sintra, where Thomas saw the palatial kitchens with huge towering heat stacks where dignitaries of many different countries were often entertained. The countryside and ocean were stunning. They had a large late lunch and a very late dinner. Dark rich Portuguese wine accompanied each meal.

On the way back to Lisbon, Thomas was surprised when Marco pulled the car off the road in the middle of nowhere, at the side of a farm field. At first, Thomas was somewhat alarmed. "Is there something wrong with the car?" he asked.

Then, Marco leaned over and gently kissed him on the cheek. Marco quietly said to Thomas, "You know, you're the person I've been looking for my whole life. I would like you to stay in Portugal and live with me. I will take good care of you."

Thomas was so shocked he didn't know what to say. He was genuinely flabbergasted. He thought about how his conservative parents were expecting him home to live with them in just two weeks and how he needed to get back to his studies at the university. Marco was so nice and generous and so deliciously handsome. Nevertheless, Thomas hadn't even confronted his own sexuality and didn't know in his own heart what all this meant. He wasn't entirely convinced that he was gay. On top of that, Marco and Thomas hadn't even been naked in front of each other and hadn't tested their chemistries.

Thomas decided that he had to say no in a way that Marco would not be upset and leave Thomas with a sour after-taste. He tried to explain to Marco, "It's impossible for me to stay and live

127

David Marty

with you. I already have other commitments. My parents are expecting me to live with them again in just weeks. It's a very generous offer and I would love to try it out but I have very little time left in Europe and I must decline."

Marco eyes began to tear. Thomas saw how much Marco loved him. By saying no, he knew he'd be breaking Marco's heart. Marco continued to plead his case as tears ran down his cheeks. "Please give it some real thought. I love you very much."

Thomas said in the most definitive manner, "I'm so sorry I must say no." Then he added, "But I've really appreciated my time with you. You are a very caring and sweet man; I think maybe I love you too."

Thomas wasn't sure, if being a kept boy was what he really wanted or if Marco was sincere about wanting a life-long companion. How long could such an arrangement last? They'd only spent a day and a half together. He didn't want to consider the possibility that Marco might only want him sexually. It seemed improbable. Neither had been sexually aroused to the point of notice. Yet Marco seemed like a mentor from whom Thomas could really learn. The physical attraction was also very strong.

After some time, Marco composed himself and reluctantly drove Thomas back to the camp. Once back, Thomas decided that he wanted to spend one more day in Lisbon, but he was afraid that Marco would find him again and try to convince him to stay.

The next morning, he found a hostel and moved his belongings there for a night. The day after that, Thomas left Lisbon. He was sad and conflicted. He folded the paper that had Marco's name, address, and phone number on it. He tucked it into his

128

wallet. Thomas, maybe for the first time, knew that he was most probably gay, or homosexual, and that it was not a choice. It was a definition. He wrote a letter home after that incident and described his day with a homosexual to his parents. He wasn't sure for whose benefit it was. Maybe, it was so that they could understand some of his experiences and think that he was still a "good boy".

XXVIII

Heading Back

The way back to Paris was, for the most part, uneventful and at times even sad. By this time, he was a professional hitch-hiker. Thomas traveled east to Badajoz, Spain. His last ride took him to the east side of that city. He was holding his hand written sign that said Madrid. He rolled out his sleeping bag and bedded down for the night. He dreamed about Marco. They were both naked and holding each other passionately. Thomas woke in a puddle of his own semen after an erotic wet dream.

The next day, Thomas had just unfurled his sign for Madrid when a car stopped. A young French woman pulled to the side of the road and stopped her car. She was very pretty, young and outgoing. She said, "I call myself Marie." She spoke only French.

He introduced himself as Thomas. He had to scurry to get his things in order. He never expected such a quick response. Thomas felt very comfortable having found a driver who spoke French. It was easier for him to converse, ask questions and answer. Thomas wasn't sure if it was luck or Providence but as they spoke, Marie told him she wasn't going to Madrid; she was

130

Liberating Tomas

going all the way to Biarritz, France. Her car was the classic Deux Chevaux, by Citroen. He had ridden in a couple of them before. It always made him laugh at the fact that the front windows didn't roll up. Instead, to raise the window, one had to fold the bottom half of the window and secure it to the window frame with a frame clip. Thomas had to go back to Bilbao to collect the items he'd left there in a storage locker. However, the long ride was a rare treat for him and Marie was a warm and friendly woman. She reminded him of his older sister back home. He could ride with Marie until the road forked with one branch to Vitoria and the other to Bilbao.

After a while, he realized that he forgot to take a bathroom break; now he really had to pee badly. He became more and more agitated and desperate. There weren't any convenience stations along the rural route. He tried to keep the French conversation going but finally pleaded with Marie to pull over so that he could do his business.

Marie was able to stop near a grassy field and Thomas ran out into an open pasture. He quickly unbuttoned his fly and started to pee like a racehorse. It was such a relief for him. He kept looking over his shoulder to make sure Marie didn't drive off with his huge backpack. He needn't have worried.

He ran back to the car and jumped in. Marie questioned him, "Are you better now?"

He replied, "Yes, thank you so much." Marie put the car into gear and continued the journey.

As night approached, Marie said in French, "I think that we should get a room at the next available spot. I'm getting too tired to drive much further and I don't like to drive at night"

Thomas agreed that it was a good idea and offered to pay half of the room rate. *Does it matter that Marie and I are not married*

131

David Marty

and that I'm only nineteen? He wondered. He was sure that it would have been a problem in 1970 in the U.S. However, maybe in Spain it was different.

They were easily able to get a small room to share. There was a common bathroom down the hall and Thomas washed himself in the shower. Back in the room, there was only one small bed and they were to share it. He had never slept with a woman before. In addition, he had no bedclothes. Marie was already under the covers so Thomas wasn't sure if she was sleeping naked. Thomas got under the covers naked and pretended to sleep. He didn't know if sexual relations were expected. If that was to happen, who was supposed to make the first move? He wasn't even sure what they would do if they did have sex and of course, there were no condoms. The fantasy of sleeping with his "sister" was disturbing to him. He lay there, wide-awake, listening to Marie breathing next to him. He wasn't interested in Marie sexually and felt that he would've been much more comfortable with another naked man. Once he was sure Marie was asleep, he fell asleep too.

By morning, they both rose early. Neither talked about the night's sleep and Thomas was relieved. They continued toward Burgos and finally made it to the fork where Marie had to turn off. They parted, he hoped, as friends.

Thomas was able to get a short ride into Bilbao where he found all the things he didn't want to drag with him to Spain and Portugal. This included his huge Duluth pack and a leather coat that he had purchased in Bilbao.

From Bilbao to San Sebastian, Thomas got a ride from another truck driver. The trucker only spoke Spanish so Tom's meager Spanish was not very helpful. He kept pointing up

132

to the hills and saying "Toro". *Thomas was sure that he didn't mean that there was a Toro lawn mower factory nearby. That factory was in Minneapolis.* Many miles later, he realized that Toro was Spanish for bull. Then he finally figured the driver picked him up because he thought that Thomas was a toreador-in-training. His red sleeping bag, leather coat, and slight physique, were classic indicators of a toreador. Thomas smiled and gestured to the man, trying to explain that he was not a bullfighter. The driver seemed to want to believe secretly that Thomas was one anyway.

He got as far as Bayonne, France, that night. It felt good being in a place where he could more easily understand the language again. He remembered sleeping in the outskirts of town where he found a dry lean-to near a laundry station. Thomas woke up in the middle of the night to see a huge jackrabbit hopping nearby. On the other hand, maybe it was a dream.

The next morning, he got a ride from a young man from Brittany, Northern France. Jean was a young thirty, slightly older than Marco was. He drove Thomas all the way to Nantes. They arrived at his house. It was picturesque with beautifully colorful chickens roaming free in the front yard. The short stone barriers acted as fences between the houses and were reminiscent of the small yards of the cottages in Wales. Jean's wife and brother were waiting to greet Jean; and Thomas watched as his driver hugged and kissed both his wife and his brother on each cheek. It seemed so warm, civil, and equal. It was an example of tenderness that was uncustomary back in America. It moved Thomas. Thomas got another ride after that to Tours and spent the night in a field nearby.

133

Chartres, France 09-14-70

Dear All,

    Having a great time in Paris. Today I saw the Sorbonne, Le Boule Miche, Montmartre and Sacre Coeur. My plane leaves here at 3:00 PM. (afternoon) but I don't know when it gets there in Minneapolis, probably five or six in the evening. Hope you

---

19 © Natalia Bratslavsky/Dreamstime.com-Vitrages of Chartres Cathedral Photo

aren't too worried about the airline situation—those that were blown up and hijacked etc. I think a charter flight is safe. I still have some shopping to do but have plenty of money. See you a few days after this arrives, I hope.

Love, Tom

XXIX

Last Hitch

The next morning was a Sunday. Thomas woke to find himself in the middle of road construction. Barricades left very little room for hitchhiking on the roadside. Tom's sign now read Paris, but for over an hour in a light rain, no one stopped. Then a car pulled over. There were three people in it. The driver was a black man and the two others were young white women. They opened one of the rear doors, waiting for Thomas to get in. When he did, they told him they'd been to a wedding in Tours and were headed back to Paris, where they all lived. When Thomas told them the address in Paris where he wanted to go, they giggled.

"That's only a few blocks away from where we're going," they said. This was to be his last hitchhiking ride in Europe!

It was a very friendly threesome, a little hung over from wedding celebrations, but lively and conversant. They attempted to include Thomas in their conversations. On the way to Paris, they stopped at Chartres to see the famous stained glass of the cathedral. The church still had the original beautiful old glass, never destroyed by the Nazis. They bought some food and headed to Paris. Thomas was on his way to

136

visit Anna and Celeste, two kids with whom he had worked in Lavardens. They invited him to stay with them and their mother and father while in Paris, waiting for his departure on the university charter flight out of Orly.

20

20 © Franky/Dreamstime.com-Arc De Triomphe-Arch of Triumph Paris, France Photo

XXX

Paris

Thomas arrived at the apartment complex of the family La Salle. He asked if one of the three people in the car call ahead to alert the family of his actual arrival. After he rang the doorbell, Mme. La Salle buzzed him in from the upper apartment. Thomas got to the sixth floor and was welcomed at their door by madame. He told her he desperately needed to use a bathroom. She showed Thomas to the washroom where he quickly stripped down and was ready to sit on the toilet when he realized that it wasn't a toilet at all, but a bidet. Now in agony, he hurriedly got dressed again and asked for the w.-c. Of course, it was all on its own, through a different door, off the hallway. Finally relieved, he went back to the washroom and took a long soothing bath. It felt so good to have the luxury of hot and cold running water and real soap.

Soon, Anna and Celeste got home and Madame La Salle cooked dinner. It was a joyful reunion. Thomas met Mr. La Salle who arrived shortly before dinner. He was an officer in the French air force. Anna, Celeste, and Thomas went into Paris each day on the train. They went shopping and ate at cafes and saw Sacre-Coeur de Montmartre, the Louvre, and the Champs

Elysée, the Obélisque, the Eiffel Tower and so many other wonderful sites. Because of his French friends, he was able to enjoy Paris as a suburbanite, not a tourist. Thomas really didn't want to leave Europe, but before very long, he knew that he would have to say good-bye.

One evening, Mme. La Salle cooked cheval, horsemeat. Actually, the rest of the family ate it raw.

Mr. LaSalle explained to Thomas, "Horsemeat is commonly eaten in France. It is considered superior to other meat and doesn't carry the same bacteria as other meat."

Thomas asked Mme. LaSalle, "Is it possible to cook my horsemeat?"

"Mais oui." She let it sizzle in a pan about forty-five seconds on each side. Then she brought it back for him to eat.

Mr. LaSalle then asked Thomas, "Would you like some whisky with your meal?" Apparently, from watching too many John Wayne movies, they assumed all Americans drank whiskey with their meals.

"Non, Je prefer du vin."

Thomas couldn't stop thinking about the kind, generous and sexy Marco. He thought about his one and only failed experience with a woman, Marie, and then the privilege of all the close contacts with men during his journeys. He admired the tenderness that men in Europe seemed to be able to have with each other. He bristled at the thought of going back home where gays were shamed and considered evil sinners, even by his own parents. Gays could be tormented, blackmailed, fired from jobs, and killed all because they somehow deserved it. He was glad he came to Europe and discovered his true nature, of which he could never feel ashamed. He had a lot of learning still to do; the many ways that men could pleasure men. Nevertheless, he was eager to discover the full range of tender male love. His trip to Europe opened up a new world for him. At last, he realized that he was a homosexual. In addition, he had direct experiences that seemed to prove that very few homosexuals were perverts on a mission to molest. More likely, they were all looking for love and acceptance for who they were. That included Thomas as well.

Thomas received a letter from his sister while he was in Paris. He was surprised to find out that mail delivery occurred twice a day. Pneumatic tubes to the various city districts routed the mail. Thomas knew that his travels had changed him dramatically. When he read the letter from his sister, her uncanny remarks surprised him.

She wrote a six-page letter describing the new things happening in her life since the end of summer.

Then she wrote, *"Well, I really miss you a lot. I can hardly wait the fifteen days. Be sure to tell us what flight and everything because Mom cannot find your flight schedule. However, I am afraid when you come home; you will not be the same. I hope you still ARE the same because I might not like you otherwise. It worries me. Dad keeps saying, 'He'll be a new man when he comes home.'"*

She continued with some other things. She even asked in a hopeful manner if Pat, the English co-worker that went along to Spain was a boy or a girl.

However, she ended her letter, *"Well anyway, I hope you haven't changed much because I love you the way you are/were? I hope you have not gotten too fat or too skinny. See you soon, Love, Sis."*

Thomas began to cry because he knew he had indeed changed. He found validity in his life from strangers when he was unable to find it at home. He worried about going home to a place he'd have to hide and always pretend to be heterosexual. Now that he knew his true nature, he was reluctant to live a lie.

It was a gut wrenching decision but Thomas decided that he had to make it. He knew it was a little late to tell his parents that he wouldn't be coming home. However, it's always better late than never. He'd been thinking about Marco every day since they said their sad goodbyes and Marco dropped him off at the campground for the last time. Thomas found his wallet and took out his passport. Tucked inside the passport was Marco's contact information. Thomas asked Mme. La Salle if he could use the phone for a long distance call. He was willing to pay the charges. She showed him where the phone was and let him dial in private. Thomas knew she didn't speak English, but Marco did. Now if only Marco would answer the phone call.

The phone rang and rang. Thomas didn't want to give up easily. He let it keep ringing. Finally, he heard Marco's voice, "Hello? This is Marco."

"Marco, it's Thomas." He began to sob. "Marco, I'm not sure exactly what love is, but I think I love you. I've thought a lot about your offer to stay with you and live in Lisbon. I want to try out your offer and accept it if you'll still have me?"

The silence was deafening. Then Marco answered, "Thomas, you've made me the happiest man alive. I was hoping and praying that you would change your mind. I am thrilled. Where are you? Would you like me to pick you up?"

"I'm still in Paris," Thomas answered. "Yes, I'd be so happy if you could arrange to pick me up. Or I could take the train down to Lisbon?"

"I will fly to Paris and bring you back to Lisbon. When is your plane supposed to leave for the States?"

"A day after tomorrow," informed Thomas. "I am staying with a family who will bring me to Orly. I could meet you somewhere at the terminal. I don't want the French family to feel responsible for my not going home to America."

"I will catch a plane and be at the main information posting board at Orly, one day after tomorrow. Look for the morning flight originating in Lisbon. I can't wait to see you again. I really love you Thomas."

Meanwhile, Thomas had to send word to his family that he wouldn't be on the plane. He struggled with how to word the telegram. He knew that his family respected work and had a strong work ethic. Thomas decided to send a sort of lie to them. The telegram read, "Won't be on plane from Paris. Got a good job. Plan to stay longer. Will write soon."

21

---

21 Orly Airport Photo 1970

XXXI

Going Home or Not

When that final day in Paris came, Mr. La Salle drove the whole family, along with Thomas, to the airport. Because of his uniform, he took Thomas straight to the front of a long line of waiting passengers and got him his boarding pass. Thomas kissed goodbye to everyone and waited for the family to move out of sight. When he could no longer see them through the crowds, Thomas changed course and searched for the main information board. When he found it, he scoured the postings and saw that an Iberian Airlines plane was due to land in thirty minutes at gate F8. He almost went to the gate, but he realized that if he didn't stay near the posting board, he might miss Marco. He sat down on a long wooden bench and waited. Only a half hour later, a radiantly handsome Marco walked down the long terminal aisle. He carried a dozen long stem red roses. Thomas rushed to him, first gave him the common European cheek-to-cheek kisses, and then kissed him deeply on the mouth as the two embraced.

This was going to be a new and different beginning for both of them. Thomas had so much to learn and Marco had so much to share. Thomas was for the most part still a virgin to gay sex and thrilled that Marco loved him for who he really was. Marco

David Marty

was satisfied that he had landed the best fish in the vast sea. Thomas was excited to have his camping adventures end and the next chapter to begin.

The two lovers flew back to Lisbon seated in first-class. On the ground, Marco hailed a taxi to take Thomas to his house. It had been a long day already and Thomas was tired. Marco showed him the shower and offered a plush white robe for him to wear after he cleaned up.

Tomas nearly melted in the warm water. He let it course from his head down to his body. The spray hit his penis and at the thought about seeing Marco naked, he sprouted an erection. He couldn't stop thinking about Marco; his erection became permanent. Tomas toweled off, draped the robe around him loosely and walked out to the bedroom with his penis straight up, full of throbbing blood.

Marco had gotten comfortable. He undressed and changed to a silk robe. He walked over to Tomas and hugged him. Both robes opened and the long warm embrace joined the two at their nipples and penises. They kissed and both pair of hands eagerly explored one another. The shower and the touch from Marco exhilarated Tomas. The robes tossed on the floor, Marco guided Tomas to the clean sheets of the large bed. It was the first time they were naked together.

Marco lifted Tomas onto the bed and with his nose, he nuzzled Tomas' scrotum. The fresh boyish scent was enough to stiffen his penis. Tomas reached down and grasped the meat and discovered that it was very similar in size, and even shape, to his own; maybe just a little bit bigger. He stroked it with his young smooth fingers and played with the foreskin, alternately retracting then fully covering the cock head. Marco began dripping precum and had to stop Tomas from bringing him to orgasm so soon.

144

They shifted positions like a choreographed ballet. Marco's lips and tongue began to massage Tomas' penis and allow Tomas to layback and easily absorb the exciting new sensation. Marco was busy swallowing the early drippings from Tomas. The drops were exquisitely sweet. The men were so engrossed in the senses that it came as an equal surprise to both when Tomas started to spew gooey white streams of semen, which at first slammed onto Marco's face until Marco capped Tomas' penis with his mouth. Marco feasted on the primal juices from young Tomas. In the heat of passion, Marco lost his resistance and shot his own load above their heads. Tomas reached the wet cream and slathered it onto his chest. It was the perfect honeymoon bedroom christening.

Both men were tired and once spent, they fell into a deep sleep covered in semen; the salty somewhat bitter and gooey taste of sperm left in Marco's mouth inspired dreams of the youthful Tomas. The two woke almost simultaneously and it was now dark in Lisbon. They playfully fondled each other; but Tomas eventually mentioned food. There would be many more moments to indulge their sexual fantasies.

Marco was somewhat embarrassed by Tomas' ragged fashion. He pledged to take Tomas shopping very soon. However, the radiant young man with the grace of a gazelle more than made up for the fashion statement of wearing shabby clothes. Marco dressed himself in a pair of crisp cotton pants and loafers. He found a sporty white cotton shirt and led Tomas down the street to his favorite Bistro.

The evening was just getting started in Lisbon. People walked or rode the public transportation to get to the many nightspots. Cars within Lisbon were not necessary and often parking was a nuisance. The food in the evening was usually

David Marty

much lighter than the noon dinner. Marco located a small table in a private area of one of his favorite restaurants. After being seating, a waiter arrived and Marco ordered an expensive bottle of wine. Tomas wasn't at all fluent in Portuguese but Marco was good about translating. The food that Marco ordered was a small platter of variety meats and sausages, grilled herring, and local cheeses. This served with crusted bread and garlic butter. It all tasted so good to Tomas because this was his first meal in ten hours.

A couple of different friends of Marco stopped by to say hello and seemed to speak approvingly of Tomas. Toward the end of the meal, a Fado guitarist sat down nearby and began to play the twelve-string guitar and sing. It was enchanting and hauntingly somber at the same time. The music echoed off the labyrinth of building facades. The musician sang a ballad from his real Portuguese experience. Tomas didn't understand any of the words.

Tomas looked closely at Marco and studied the handsome man he'd chosen to live with. It seemed as if he'd entered a fairy tale and could finally allow himself to dream of living happily ever after. He also saw a much searched for gay role model in Marco. Someone he could look up to and emulate. Tomas was again getting sleepy but wanted more naked play with Marco before the night was over.

It was only about 1 AM but Marco understood that the day had been a full one. He and Tomas walked into the night that soon found themselves back at the flat. They undressed and Marco invited Tomas to cuddle under the down quilt. Marco kissed him gently on the lips. Then with passion building, he opened Tomas' mouth and explored the young fine teeth with his tongue. Tomas became erect and Marco's hand helped to

146

pump even more blood into his shaft. With all the blood going into his penis, Tomas felt light-headed. Marco kept kissing him tenderly, while at the same time, he straddled over Tomas. His right hand found the small jar of cream that he had strategically placed on the bureau. He dabbed some onto Tomas' cock and then placed a little on his anus.

Continuing the kisses, Marco very slowly slid down on Tomas' shaft until the full length of Thomas' penis impaled him. Tomas was exquisitely sensitive to the warm muscular anus engulfing his cock. He wondered if it felt as good to Marco. He got his answer when Marco began moaning with pleasure. Marco glided up and down the shaft, milking Tomas' penis in the most erotic way. Tomas could feel every squeeze of Marco's anal muscles. That tightness really propelled Tomas toward orgasm. In the meantime, the head of Tomas' penis kept passing over Marco's prostate. Marco could feel the juices congregating for a grand reunion from the internal massage.

Tomas kept feeling his warm penis. The heat from the friction was seductive. After savoring as much heat, friction, sliding and juiciness, as he could handle, Tomas began to spew impulse after impulse of seminal fluids into Marco. Marco could feel the hot semen splash into his rectum and even without touching himself; it caused him to shoot his load all over Tomas' stomach. He slipped off the penis and the two lay in a bundle with Marco's sticky juices fusing them into one. An aroma of sex filled the entire room.

After a long pause, Tomas began to wonder what it would be like if their roles had been reversed. He was anxious to take the other role but he knew that they would have many more times to try new things. He fell asleep having sweet dreams.

David Marty

22 © Haircutting/Dreamstime.com-A View Part of the City Lisbon and Tejo River Photo

XXXII

Fitting In

The next morning was truly a new dawn. Marco was already up and getting himself ready for his workday. Tomas lay lazily wondering what he was going to do all morning without Marco. Marco came out of the bathroom and smiled at Tomas. Tomas rubbed his sleepy eyes, encouraging blood to flow into them.

Marco announced, "As I told you yesterday, I have to go to work. I'll be home around 2:00 for siesta. I'll give you a key to the flat and you can walk around and get a feel for the neighborhood. You'll be quite safe. Write my address on a paper so you won't get lost." He added, "There is fresh fruit in the fridge as well as bread and yogurt. Help yourself. Today is Marta's day off, otherwise she would make you breakfast."

Marco bent down to give Tomas a kiss goodbye and then he was off. Tomas rolled out of bed and found himself alone in the quiet two-story apartment. From the upstairs window, he could see some young children playing in a small park below. He heard some birds singing in the trees near the house. Then he walked naked to the front room. The view of the Tagus River was a wide expanse of amazing blue. The building sat on a rise about one hundred fifty feet above the river basin. The water

149

David Marty

spread out as far as the eye could see. Far away was the opposite shoreline. Daunted by all that had happened to him in the last twenty-four hours, he breathed deeply and grounded himself in his new reality.

He showered and couldn't help but smile at the clumps of dry semen that clung to the fine hairs of his body. He soaped his genitals and got stiff again thinking about the sex with Marco. He'd never felt so alive in his manhood. After rinsing, he toweled off and got dressed. Then he went to the kitchen for something to eat. Tomas picked out an orange and found some yogurt. He wasn't sure it was yogurt because it was in a large bowl without wrappers. However, the taste was telling. He sectioned the fruit and added yogurt to it in a small bowl. He didn't know how to use the coffee maker so he decided to get a cup along the way.

He spent a few minutes sleuthing through the cupboards and pantry to learn where the dishes were and where they kept various food. There wasn't a lot of food stored. Buying groceries probably was an everyday chore. A pile of escudos in bills of various denominations sat on the kitchen table. Marco really meant to take care of him! He put the bills in his wallet and made sure he had the key. Then he locked the door and walked out onto the street in front of him.

It was a glorious morning with bright sunshine and moderate temperature. The street led down to a small commercial area. He found a quaint café and sat at an outside table. When the waiter arrived, Tomas half-spoke and half-mimed that he wanted a cup of coffee. When the waiter returned with a steaming cup, he also brought a tray of assorted fresh pastries and Tomas chose one. Tomas noted how handsome the waiter was and decided that the Portuguese had much physical beauty to share with the world.

150

Liberating Tomas

Tomas sat back and watched the culture moving around him. There wasn't much vehicle traffic. Most people were on foot. Hardly anyone was fat. All the people seemed to be on a private mission but also seemed to be leisurely taking their time to accomplish the mission. Tomas noticed many people seemed to have a quiet determination and a politeness that seemed refreshing. He witnessed them eagerly help one another when they could. There was a solidarity of cohesion, which could be felt.

Tomas also wondered what he was going to write to his parents. They would most certainly disapprove of his new life. Nevertheless, this was his new life. He had to live it for himself, not for his parents.

Tomas found an old newspaper in a pile of reading material that was almost two months old. He picked it up but realized he couldn't read even the most basic words. There was one picture of Salazar, the Portuguese dictator, and another showing a horse drawn carriage holding his coffin. In the photo, military bodyguards surrounded his casket; they also cordoned off crowds of people from direct contact with him.

Tomas mentally started a list of things he wanted to ask Marco later on. Tomas noted very few young men his age. He observed how they walked together and how they were dressed. Tomas couldn't help but to undress the younger men in his young and wild mind. Most of the pedestrians were dressed in tailored clothes or European jeans wearing sturdy but stylish shoes. It reminded Tomas of the fashions of London with the influences of the Beatles. He wanted to blend into the culture swiftly so that he wouldn't stand out so much. He envied the wide flared legs of the pants. It made the men's buttocks seem even more perky and delightful.

151

David Marty

Sitting on the other side of the cafe were three older women who seemed to be passing the time together sipping tea. They were dressed in dark drab utilitarian dresses. They were busy knitting, crocheting, and talking back and forth. After noon, they got up together and left, probably to go to their respective homes to make dinner for their men.

Tomas found a haberdashery nearby and decided to look inside. A clerk approached him right away but Tomas motioned that he was only looking. A mannequin dressed in a beautiful thick red sweater stood out from all the other displays. The sweater was a cardigan, buttoning down the front. It had a cowl neck and was thick enough to keep him cozy and warm in the Portuguese winter that would be coming soon. Tomas really resonated with it. He counted his money and realized that the clothes in this shop were expensive. On the other hand, they seemed to have the quality that could exact a higher price.

He came across a flower shop and decided to use some of the money to buy flowers for Marco. He picked a variety of different colorful flowers. Then he bounded up the hill and back to the flat.

Tomas sat down in the living room; and looked at a photo album left on the table near the settee. It pictured Marco at a young age as well as Marco's mother and sister. He was wondering about Marco's father. All of a sudden, a young woman entered the apartment without knocking.

Marta walked in and startled Tomas. She immediately introduced herself, "I am Marta. I didn't mean to scare you."

Tomas replied, "Marco told me it was your day off."

"It is my day off, but Marco told me about your arrival and I thought that it would be appropriate to cook a welcome dinner in your honor," she politely answered. "Nothing too fancy, but

152

I was at the fish market and bought the makings for a hearty Portuguese fish stew."

Tomas decided that she was in her early thirties. Marta had dark hair, dark eyes and a sensuous mouth. Her pale skin, like alabaster, seemed to illuminate her face. She was slim and buxom yet her plain clothing concealed her with modesty. Tomas was very interested in cooking, so he asked, "Can I watch you and maybe help?"

"Of course. You don't have to, but you are certainly welcome to help me," she replied. It was just then that Tomas realized that Marta was speaking English.

"I want to learn Portuguese too, if you have the patience to teach me."

"I will gradually work in Portuguese as we cook and converse. I'm quite patient, but you don't need to know everything all at once. I teach English as a second language twice–a–week."

Tomas expected total immersion but was grateful that Marta would go slowly. He followed her into the kitchen and helped her to unpack the groceries. In one white butcher's bag, there was a snake-like creature. Marta explained that it was an eel and made a tasty addition to the fish stew. He mostly watched as Marta prepared each item, naming them one by one in Portuguese. The stew she made contained tomatoes, potatoes, onions, and a variety of fish, clams, shrimp and eel. The large pot was filled to almost overflowing. She covered it and let it simmer. It would be ready in about two hours, when Marco was going to be home.

Marco arrived just after 2:00 and greeted Tomas with a kiss right in front of Marta. She smiled. It was good to see Marco happy. Marco invited Marta to join them for dinner. The fish stew was delicious. Warm bread with butter was the only accompaniment. Tomas dipped his bread into the bowl to sop up the

David Marty

delicious broth. When they'd all finished, Marta cleared the dishes and was busy washing them in the kitchen. Marco looked at Tomas and asked him about his day so far.

Tomas recounted his limited exposure to the neighborhood. He mentioned that the young men seemed very sexy and exotic to him, but there seemed to be very few of them. Tomas also told Marco about the slacks and sweater he saw at the clothing store. Marco insisted on going with Thomas that evening to pick out some new clothes.

Tomas asked quite bluntly, "Why are there so few men around my age walking on the streets?"

Marco informed Tomas, "Portugal conscripts almost all men eighteen to twenty-three for military service. Some men are stationed here to maintain order. Many other soldiers are sent to Angola, Mozambique and the other colonies. Many young men who don't want to serve in the military emigrate illegally to France and Great Britain, even to Brazil."

Tomas could tell that Marco was interested to telling him the best side of Portugal, avoiding any disgust he had with the current regime. He looked deep into Marco's eyes and saw them gleam when Marco suggested they take a nap. Marta was already finishing up and stopped long enough to say goodbye on her way out. As soon as the door closed, Tomas undressed entirely and began to parade around the dining room table naked, as if he was Marilyn Monroe. He felt Marco's gaze and that encouraged him to get an erection.

It took a little more time for Marco to lose his clothes but when he did, he walked up to Tomas and placed his fingers around the shaft of Tomas' penis. Marco himself was also erect. Tomas bent over and displayed his perfect boyish rear end to Marco. Marco bent down and slid his tongue down the crack

154

between Tomas' glutei. Then, Tomas began to feel the incredible sensual sensation of Marco's tongue slithering around his anus and attempting to enter his hole. Tomas felt so good. They waltzed into the bedroom and half stumbled into bed. They held each other's penises and gazed intently into one another's eyes. They warmly embraced and kissed deeply.

Tomas asked Marco, "Does it hurt?"

"Does what hurt?"

"Does it hurt when you sit on my penis and it goes all the way inside you?"

Marco grinned, "It hurts just a little, right in the beginning. However, once the head of your penis opens me, it starts to feel good, very good, and wonderful in fact! I feel a close attachment that is indescribable. When your penis head strokes my prostate and I feel your thick throbbing warm shaft, it feels out of this world."

Tomas was getting super hard listening to Marco. He asked, "Will you penetrate me?"

Marco cautioned that Tomas would have to relax enough so that Marco could enter. Marco put his index finger to Tomas' hole. It was the tight hole of a young virgin. He massaged the anal area and gently poked the tip of his finger into the hole. He withdrew and added some lubricant to the finger. With a quick poke, his finger was through the sphincter and into Tomas.

Tomas winced at the new intrusion. However, as Marco's finger slid deeper into his bowel, Tomas felt a fullness he'd never even dreamt of before. Marco's finger found Tomas' prostate and began to massage it lightly. Tomas felt his penis swell from the internal stimulation. After a few minutes, Marco pulled his finger away. Tomas was disappointed.

Marco helped Tomas get onto his back and raised his legs, holding onto Tomas' ankles. Marco's fully ridged erection begged at the back door. He put the tip of his penis directly in contact with Tomas' anus and teased the opening of the hole. Before very long, Tomas was pleading with Marco to enter him. With the addition of some lubrication, Marco delicately penetrated the outer ring of Tomas' rectum. Tomas gave a small whimper. Then Marco slowly and cautiously pushed his hard penis deeper and deeper into Tomas.

Tomas felt the initial entrance. It really hurt, a little. Marco pushed slow enough that Tomas had time to relax and now he could feel Marco becoming part of him inch by inch. It felt so much better than the finger, softer with a warm pulsating full girth. Tomas could feel the swelling of this warm thick appendage and marveled at the glorious fit it seemed to have. The initial pain soon gave way to amazing fullness. Marco was adept at using Tomas' legs as levers to pull and push his penis in and out of Thomas. Together, they developed a gentle synchronous rhythm.

Marco hadn't copulated like this in a long time. Tomas was enjoying his deflowering. The two attached as one; the warm wildly plowed sensations intensified the action. Tomas yelled to Marco, "You're going to force an orgasm out of me!"

Just a few more strokes over his prostate and Tomas started having prolonged orgasmic spasms. From his own penis, Marco felt Tomas' prostate contracting, churning the load inside of him. As Tomas' rectal muscles began to spasm in ecstasy, Marco let his own load shoot deep inside Tomas. Tomas felt the warm sperm squirt into his intestines. At the same moment, Tomas shot his own load, which ricocheted off Marco's abdomen, then dripped back onto his own stomach.

Wow! Tomas had no idea that this could be so dramatic. He knew of nothing that compared. He'd always wondered what it was like to internalize germinal fluids with another man. In some primeval context, his juices had earlier become a part of Marco and now Marco's own juices collided in his colon.

Marco wanted to stay attached for a long time. It was a bond he never wanted broken. Nevertheless, Tomas slowly began to expel Marco's shaft. As the head popped out, semen dripped out as well. Marco had amassed such a huge overflowing load that Tomas' sphincter couldn't contain all of it. Marco cleaned his penis with a wet towel and wiped up the fluids on Tomas' belly and anus. They fell into sleep entwined in each other's arms.

Leaving Tomas sound asleep, Marco dressed and returned to work. He left a note: "Tomas, I'll be home at seven. Make yourself comfortable. We can go clothes shopping when I return."

Tomas knew that his telegram would have arrived at his parents' by now, saying he wouldn't be on the plane from Paris. Tomas also speculated that his mother would be worried. He knew his older brother was going to register him for the next semester at university. It was to start the week following Tom's return home. It wasn't like Tom, his mother's favorite son, to neglect following through with his plans. He didn't explain why he would take a job when he should be in school.

Tomas knew that he'd have to write a longer letter soon to address some of his parents' concerns. He wondered why he'd written about meeting a homosexual. It was sure to start the wheels turning in Paul's brain. Tomas would have to mail a letter soon, knowing that it might take more than a week to arrive. Tomas knew it would be a burden for his mother and father to try to explain his no-show to others. Then he wondered about the pewter

David Marty

lamp that he mailed home. The flimsy cardboard box covered with brown wrapping paper seemed unlikely to make it all the way home safely.

Tomas woke up and immediately focused on the feeling that Marco's penis was still inside of him. He smiled and expelled a small amount of Marco's semen that had migrated to his anal opening. What a wonderfully wild experience. Not one to dilly-dally, Tomas got up, showered again and dressed. He found Marco's note and became anxious to go shopping. He decided to go back to the café, which he'd discovered that morning. This time when he looked down the street toward the commercial docks, he could see a row of men in drab military uniforms. It appeared that each one had an automatic weapon. Tomas shivered because it had the look and feel of intimidation.

While he sat and watched, the thought of his letter home kept encroaching into his mind. Tomas wondered if he should tell the truth or continue the imaginative story about a job. He decided that the job angle would be easier for his mother and father to accept. He began drafting a letter. Tomas made up a company name and decided he would use his real Lisbon address, in care of Marco. Tomas jotted on some paper that his new job was a French and English interpreter working for the international company, Vandelay Industries, headquartered in Lisbon. He was going to be paid $5,000/year plus his expenses. The job was six months long at least; subject to review with a possibility of becoming full time after that. He read it and re-read it. He decided that it was credible enough. The sun was just beginning to set and Tomas hurried home where he was able to see the sun fade behind the western hills.

158

Marco arrived after seven. He hugged and kissed Tomas. Tomas grinned and announced, "I can still feel you inside of me. It was awesome."

Marco smiled and was inwardly happy that Tomas had so much enjoyment. He offered, "Let me change my clothes and we'll go shopping!"

Tomas picked out a few things: flared-leg slacks, shirts with wide collars, socks and underwear. The Beatles and their fashion had arrived in Portugal ahead of America. When there seemed to be a conflict in choices, Marco helped him make wise decisions. Tomas pointed to the red sweater on the mannequin and said to Marco, "I really like the red sweater."

Marco smiled and told Tomas, "Red is the color of the communists. In Lisbon, wearing red is uncommon. The authorities do not appreciate the color, but if you really like it, I'll get it for you. Because you're an American, they probably won't give you any trouble."

Marco paid the bill and they went home. They both undressed and moved to the bed. They cuddled and Tomas squeezed Marco's well-developed glutei muscles. Marco returned the favor and they fell asleep on the edge of orgasm.

XXXIII

The New Order

Sex between the young man and his older consort was frequent, diverse, and totally fulfilling for both parties. It soon became apparent to them that they could effectively communicate their sexual needs and desires just by using body language and eye contact. Tomas was still at an age that any sexual fantasy might lead to an erection. An invigorated Marco relished the youthful playfulness that Tomas brought to his all too serious life. He could leave his problems behind and become free of most of his worldly concerns. For both of them, the frequent sex was leading to a renewed vitality with an increase in energy.

Tomas was fretting over his letter that he planned to send to his parents. He finally decided to let Marco read his draft. Marco, a caretaker by nature, was happy to assist Tomas. Reading the proposed letter, Marco politely told Tomas that his letter should be even more credible than what he had written so far.

"Why don't you tell them that you work with me at Holiday Inn, Portugal? I can have you entered as an employee and it will seem legitimate. Then if your father decides to check, it will look perfectly normal."

He added, "I think you should say your salary is $10,000 a year."

Tomas liked the ideas and reframed his letter, mailing it the next day. Now his father and mother would have a way to get a hold of him either by mail or phone. He figured they would still be anxiously inquisitive, but at least the ball was now back in their court.

Tomas sometimes felt over-dressed in his new European clothes but he liked his new look. September was a bit too warm for him to wear his new sweater. He was a fast learner of Portuguese and Marta was a steady teacher. Marta worked five days a week for Marco. She ran the kitchen and tended to most of the housework and laundry. She often took Tomas to the big Mercado da Ribeira and together, they shopped for locally grown fruits and vegetables. Tomas asked many questions about her cooking. He was surprised to find out that she was very knowledgeable of the nutrients found in each food and the methods to prepare and augment nutrition.

Marta decided that Tomas should learn Portuguese history as well as the language. Over the course of the next year, she tutored Tomas. Marta seduced and beguiled him by her command of both language and history.

Tomas was impressed with Portugal. Its obscurity on the western peninsula of Iberia forced it to create a unique identity. He learned from Marta that Portugal was not isolated in the usual sense. First inhabited by the Iberians, they knew it as Lusitania. Then there was an influx from the Celts. Later the Goths, the Moors, and the Romans also conquered it. Spain at times dominated the whole peninsula. In World War I, Portugal fought with England. During World War II, Portugal remained neutral,

161

courting the favor of both sides. Historically, all invaders either assimilated or left the country.

Portugal remained provincial. When most of Europe was progressing into the industrial revolution, Portugal remained agrarian because it lacked coal to fuel new industries. Yet there weren't large tracts of land to farm. With all the steep hills and deep valleys, Portugal developed a system of agriculture that was labor intensive. Many different crops grew because of the abundance of microclimates surrounding the rugged terrain. The sloping fields etched into land of different terraces could support unique varieties of crops.

Marta enriched Tomas' experience by taking him to some of the many museums and historical sites, which Lisbon had to offer. At Restauradores Square, in Baixa, Tomas learned of how Portugal was the leader of ocean exploration in the 1500's. Sailors such as Vasco de Gama, Fernao de Magalhhaes (Magellan), Afonso de Albuquerque, Pedro Alvares Cabral, Prince Henry the Navigator, and others explored South America, India, China, East Africa, and Japan. According to Marta, they were instructed by the royales to bring back samples of flora and fauna which were studied and coaxed to grow in Portugal. Tomatoes, corn, melons, from the New World, and all the exotic spices of India along with lemons and oranges from the orient became a part of the national treasure.

On another field trip, Marta and Tomas rode the #15W trolley to Belem. They arrived at the Moorish Castle, Castelo Sao Jorge the Moors. Marta guided Tomas almost exclusively in Portuguese and told him that the site dated back to 48 BC. The Moors invaded Portugal in 711, and were an Islamic force in some parts of the country for over five centuries. The Christians and Islamic forces battled each other for many of those centuries.

Beginning in the seventh and eighth centuries, the Moors were defeated and there was a re-establishment of Christianity. There were many local counts and regional kings. The Roman pope acknowledged the first king of Portugal and Christianity became entrenched into the culture with clergy and popes calling most of the shots. The royals intermarried, often with other European monarchs.

By 1494, Manuel the first became king. He presided over the discovery of India as his immediate predecessor did over the New World discoveries. Proclaimed king in 1707, Dom Joao V became the wealthiest monarch in Europe of his time, because of all the riches discovered in Brazil. In 1755, a powerful earthquake destroyed a third of Lisbon and killed 12,000 people. The royal residences were toppled. It was the most devastating earthquake ever in Europe, and caused destructive tsunamis as far away as Martinique. The Marquis of Pombal emerged to rebuild much of Lisbon in a modern, grid style pattern of wide avenues. He also modernized Portugal's industry, agriculture and finances, expelled the Jesuits, reduced the power of the nobility, and took away privileges of foreign traders.

In November 1807, France invaded Lisbon. As the invasion was happening, the royal family, its entourage, the government administrative hierarchy, and supporters decided to leave Portugal. At least ten thousand people escaped to Brazil in a flotilla, using any available sea worthy ships. Then, the monarchy ruled Portugal from Brazil for nearly 100 years.

The nineteenth century was a period of conflicts between supporters of the monarchy, social liberals, constitutionalists and republicans. In 1908, a revolution began when King Dom Carlos and his older son, Dom Luis Filipe were assassinated. The younger son, Dom Manuel II assumed the throne but by 1910, he

David Marty

abdicated and fled to England. That was the end of Portugal's monarchy.[23]

Marta knew so many of the stories but much of the history was complicated for Tomas. He ventured back on his own to many of the museums to try to comprehend the many aspects of Portuguese history. Lisbon seemed to have history around every corner. Tomas found it incredulous knowing that Portugal was the richest country of the word at the same time that the America's were only being discovered. The peak greatness of Portugal also overlapped with the Inquisition and the Black Plague. It was no wonder that there were ready volunteers to sail uncharted oceans.

Tomas asked about the dictator Salazar. He died less than two months earlier. Marta tried to educate Tomas about the Portugal of the twentieth century. However, she made the comment, "As for Salazar, keep your eyes open. Many people liked him for preserving Portugal, but the cost in human rights, especially for women and gays is difficult to tolerate."

The history of Portugal was rich with heroes and adventurers. Many of its Kings were poets because only the elite received education. It was from all those riches that children of Portugal viewed their role models and chose the people they wanted to emulate and on which to imprint. It was a much more sincere upbringing than watching heroes on television and movies. Marco chose many role models to mimic but his father was probably his strongest immediate role model.

---

23 Paraphrase from Jose Hermano Saraiva, Portugal A Companion History, Carcanet Press Limited 1997

Dear Tom,

Just a short letter. Of course, we got your telegram. Thank you for sending it. We also got your letter and we're pleased that you have a well-paying job. Your father and I are very worried about you. Your brother enrolled you at University but now you won't be attending this fall. We don't even know what to tell our friends. Maybe you can clarify things. It seems like you have landed a good job but it isn't like you to suspend your studies. By the way, I received a package from Portugal. I shook the box a little and heard the noise of crackling sand. When I opened the package, there was a pewter lamp base but sadly, the glass shade was in a thousand pieces. I hope you are well and happy. Please keep us in your thoughts and prayers, as we will also do for you. Write to us.

Love, Mom

P.S. I'm sorry to have to tell you but your dog, Shadow died last week. He lived a good long life but he seemed heartbroken since you left home.

XXXIV

Mending Wounds

Tomas quietly mourned Shadow's passing. His mother certainly had a way to guilt him. However, he was pleasantly surprised that the letter from his mother was short and didn't contain any condemnation. Now that they had his new address and phone number, he expected a phone call. Lisbon was six hours ahead of Minneapolis so a call from home would probably come in the evening. It seemed most likely that there would be no one to answer it. Hardly anyone in Lisbon answered the phone at night because of dictatorship fears. Nearly any conversation might be listened to. Evenings were times people went out for supper, listen to Fado music or the radio. Tomas dreaded talking to his parents directly because he was a bad liar and he didn't want to give voice to falsehoods.

During the first weekend after Tomas arrived in Marco's home, Marco drove Tomas around the outskirts of Lisbon. He was proud to show Tomas some of the most beautiful parts of the country. They ate at a couple of small restaurants with outdoor seating. It was reminiscent of their very first encounters. Tomas resurrected his habit of smoking Galois cigarettes and Marco smoked as well. The many people they met seemed to be

166

struggling; yet somehow they seemed adept at overcoming most of the more backward aspects of Portuguese life. Marco promised to show Tomas the ocean beaches when the heat of summer returned.

Marco hoped that Tomas would learn Portuguese, yet he often spoke to others in his mother tongue when he didn't want Tomas to know about the exact conversation. It was an incentive for Tomas to learn the language as fast as possible.

Tomas was impressed with Marco's body. For a mature man of twenty-seven, Marco was in very fit shape. Marco was strong, muscular and sexy. Tomas' body had the perfection of youth. Tomas had built up his buttocks during his formative high school days by running hurdles in track. He also worked many physically taxing jobs in his young life. His muscles rippled under his tight skin and his proportions and inner structure were flawless. Together, they made a beautiful pair of males. Tomas liked to run his fingers through Marco's coarse wavy hair. Marco enjoyed looking through Tomas' brown eyes and into his soul as Tomas held his head. The two seemed perfect for each other.

Tomas experienced sex in new ways nearly every time they were naked together. He enjoyed being both dominant and submissive. It took trust and admiration to be on both sides of sex. Tomas not only felt free to try anything but ultimately felt his sexual being had finally been liberated without equivocation.

As the days went on, Tomas began to explore his new city. He sometimes wandered the narrow cobblestone streets as if he was a mouse in a maze. The closeness of the buildings often made him feel claustrophobic. Then he would reach the end of a block and walk into a small park or an overlook where he could expand

David Marty

his vista to other vast parts of the city. The city was multi-layered. The different hills hosting the seventeenth century buildings were often the demarcations of neighborhoods.

From Baixa, Tomas could walk to the quaint street elevator of Santa Justa and ascend from the lower streets of Chiado to the higher Largo do Carmo. The possibilities were endless whether to take the subway, the electric tram, the funiculars, or the buses. Many of the streets were only wide enough to carry public transportation. Small personal cars usually deferred to one-way streets. Lisboans tried to be courteous to leave room for vehicular and pedestrian traffic while parking their bikes, mopeds, or small cars on the narrow streets. Parking was at a premium but some blocks offered underground spaces for residents.

At first, Tomas walked almost everywhere. It was very challenging to stroll stone streets that often seemed to be endless uphill corridors. While his young legs were strong, he became increasingly comfortable using public transit as his area of adventure increased.

Marta and Tomas often rode the 15E tram together when they went to Mercado da Ribeira for produce. It was a huge farmer's and flea market. Tomas sometimes stood back and watched Marta negotiate prices and hand- pick different items. He also observed her sometimes taking a little longer with certain merchants and she seemed to be exchanging more than just greetings and money. After several trips to the market, Tomas realized that many of the booths where Marta lingered longer displayed a small bouquet of red flowers either on their table or in the back part of their booths.

One day, Tomas surprised Marta and asked, "Is there some significance to having red flowers on display?"

168

Marta was somewhat flustered by his directness. "There is a significance. Those supporters of the resistance often display red flowers as a show solidarity."

Tomas naively asked, "Resistance to what exactly?"

Marta then decided he should know. She started, "Salazar has been dictator so long, that he has created many enemies. Many of the women, artists, liberals, socialist, and even communists are working to topple the regime and restore basic civil rights. You probably have noticed that there are no actual police officers on the streets. There are soldiers with automatic weapons acting as police, the PIDE, and then there are the secret police, the PVDE. The PVDE is modeled after the Gestapo and you do not want them to be watching you if you can help it. You must be very careful not to talk against the regime in public. Even the telephones are not secure. I lost my father to the Salazar regime. Stationed in Mozambique, he caught Malaria and died. I have some personal hostility toward the Salazar dictatorship."

"But Salazar is dead now," countered Tomas.

Marta continued, "He has been 'dead' and incapacitated for over two years now, His actual death hasn't changed anything. If anything, things have gotten worse. But we, in the resistance, want to work for the final push to liberation, now that he is completely out of the picture."

Tomas gulped. He really didn't know very much about Salazar and his impact on Portugal and its people. He was surprised that Marta had taken an active role in the resistance. His curiosity was piqued and he wanted to know a lot more.

Marta then divulged, "I help inform people of the meetings and goals when I am here in the market. I am an organizer and presenter for some of those meetings. That is why I talk a little

David Marty

longer to some of the merchants. They are friends. You must be very careful who you talk to about the resistance."

Tomas decided not to ask any more questions right then and the two hopped back onto the 15E to get back to Marco's place.

XXXV

Marco's Story

On Marco's birthday, October 11, Marco said to Tomas, "I want you to join me for a wonderfully romantic evening out at a restaurant tonight." The late evening meal was modest and very good. It was a warm evening and they finished dessert seated on the outdoor patio of the restaurant, overlooking lower parts of the city. Marco ordered a bottle of port wine and they sipped the wine admiring each other. They were a handsome couple and the small age difference between the two seemed to evaporate.

Tomas broke the silence by saying, "Marco, you know a lot about me but I know hardly anything about you. Tell me about your life and how you got to be twenty-eight."

Marco started, "It's a long story. I'll begin with some background. My father came from Germany. He fled his homeland at the beginning of the war and came to live in Portugal, which was neutral during WWII. He was educated as a physician and started to practice medicine in Lisbon."

"My father immigrated to Portugal in 1939. Germany was getting unbearable and he took a seldom-used route to escape Hitler's control. My father had just finished medical school and observed the harsh treatment that his Jewish friends received by

David Marty

the Nazis. Being educated and fair-minded, he also felt helpless to change the situation. He heard that Portugal was looking for educated medical doctors and was recruiting. Dad jumped at the opportunity to leave Germany."

"At the age of twenty-four, my father settled in the center of Lisbon. He enjoyed Portuguese life. Buildings, customs and culture seemed stuck in the past. He once confided in me that he found the young women fascinatingly beautiful."

"After about a year practicing medicine in a hospital, my father met Angela. She was pure Portuguese and very smart and beautiful. Unlike many women, my mother finished parochial school and trained as a nursing assistant. The two made a good pair; and soon they married. I was born in October 1943. My younger sister, Teresa, was born in 1945."

*   *   *

Once the war was over, Salazar regained his footing but now became worried, even paranoid, about Communism triumphing in a weakened Europe. Salazar became friendlier with General Franco of Spain even though Salazar also detested Fascism. Franco was much more militaristic and had blindly bombed his own people during the Spanish Civil War. Salazar was an economist and relied on his security forces to maintain civil control. Salazar's local police, the PIDE, appeared throughout the city to intimidate citizens so they would follow the conservative order. Their presence discouraged most crime and kept people docile. Keeping people in poverty was another guarantee that rebellion would be limited. He also had his secret police, the PVDE. These secret police were in charge of stifling and smothering any leftist dissent.

After the war, these secret police ramped up their power. They began to take dissidents away from their homes in the middle of the night, arrest them, and torture them until they gave up secrets in order to compile a full list of active resistance members. When the prisoners survived the torture, they were often exiled to remote Portuguese territories. Any conversation that contained criticism of the government was forbidden and often ruthlessly punished.

* * *

Marco continued, "My parents had a comfortable life, even though my father Werner often worked with very poor people. He sometimes treated people free, other times he traded for services. My mother, Angela, was devoted to Werner and often worked as his receptionist. They developed a small circle of friends. Having seen what happened under Hitler, my father felt obligated to sympathize with the cause of those who spoke against the dictatorship. Many of his patients had grievances. The more people the regime locked away and tortured, the more the resistance grew. People spied on each other and informants often implicated innocent friends because of personal grudges.

One night, I heard the PVDE's ominous sirens climbing up through the cobblestone streets and stop at our house. I watched from my bedroom window as security men in trench coats abducted my father. I never saw or heard from him again him. They had taken so many others, to an unknown location with an unknown fate. I was only thirteen. It was the last time I saw my father."

Tomas was astounded. His eyes grew wide as he tried to comprehend. He had no reference for brutal dictatorial tactics. He

David Marty

wasn't sure what to say to Marco. He asked, "What happened after that?"

Marco continued, "My mother was devastated. She was alone with her two children, my sister Teresa and myself. She no longer had a source of income and she decided the best thing to do would be to move us to the countryside where her mother, Luisa, lived and things were less expensive."

"We moved to Sao Joao and I continued my schooling at a parochial school. At first, I was bored living in the country. The people had bigger detached houses and yards but seemed poorer. Everyday life was a struggle and people worked together in small groups and extended families to insure an adequate level of existence. There were many chores for a teenager. Taking care of the animals and tending the large gardens was a chance to have healthy fresh food. Luisa, my grandmother, taught me to weed the gardens. It was grueling work but soon my muscles grew to handle it. Grandmamma would dig around the roots of a wilting plant and find a cutworm. I would watch as she put it in her mouth, cut it in half with her teeth and then spit it onto the ground."

"As a teenage boy, they asked me to participate in the round up and slaughter of the pigs. Several friends and I ran and chased a pig that was squealing and wild. When we caught the pig, an older man came and slit the pig's throat. In Portugal, pigs are valuable and utilization of all parts of it is economical. Someone would singe off the thick hair bristles so the skin could be crisped and eaten. I can still smell the scent of burning hair. Other cuts of the pig were either salted or smoked. Thoroughly washed intestines stuffed with small pieces of meat made the smoked sausage, chouico."

"I was keenly observant of animal life. I had no bias toward animals having sex for fun or for procreation. It all seemed normal to me. I made a few friends, and as boys often do, we played together and experimented with sex. It was a part of the rite of passage. I always got excited to watch and touch my boyhood playmates. "

"While I enjoyed the expanses of the country, I missed the energy of Lisbon. It was the only city able to keep up a pace with the rest of Europe. I was lonesome much of the time and devoted my free time to helping my mother and sister adjust to life without Dad. I became even more of a caretaker."

"At sixteen, I was just beginning to become a man. In high school, I made a new friend, Carlos. We were the same age and we enjoyed exploring each other and comparing our bodies. We often went to Costa da Caparica in the summer. At the most remote end of the long beach, there was a gay clothing optional section. Many times, we made love on the sand, between sheets. Once we were so preoccupied that we didn't notice that a group of somewhat older men had congregated around our sheet. After we finished, many of the men ejaculated and semen rained down on us. I'll never forget that day. We had many wonderful erotic times together. Carlos was also a real friend that I could confide in. Neither he nor I had many sexual role models to mimic. When we turned eighteen, we became eligible for conscription."

"Wait," Tomas implored. "I just found out that I'm in line to be drafted to go to Viet Nam. Why does Portugal have a draft?"

"Men are drafted and deployed to the colonies of Portugal. My good friend, Carlos, got the call. I decided I didn't want to be a part of the army. A priest from school helped me to flee illegally to England. He found a work-study program for me in

David Marty

London and I began to learn about the hospitality industry. I became fluent in English and I worked at Holiday Inn, London.

* * *

By the early 1960's, forty percent of Portugal's impoverished economy went to manage the colonies. The United Nations often chastised Portugal for maintaining those colonies. Portugal's defense was always that these scattered lands were part of Portugal itself and not separate colonies. In any case, Portugal was using a large part of its feeble economy to maintain them. Also by 1960, Salazar realized there were so many disgruntled citizens of Portugal he would have to do more to placate the masses. He opened up Portugal for foreign investment but restricted profits from leaving the country. He decided to fund education on a much higher level, and built secondary, vocational/technical, and university infrastructure. Portugal was actually making strides to catch up to the rest of the world. Unfortunately, for Salazar, the more he gave to the people, the more they realized what he had withheld from them for so long. He could always count on loyalty from the conservative National Union Party. Nevertheless, he was losing support from a moderating Catholic Church.

In 1968, Salazar suffered a brain hemorrhage. Expected to die, the regime handpicked Marcello Caetano to replace him. When Salazar regained lucidity, he thought he was still privately ruling Portugal. He died July 29, 1970. Those who loved him, those who hated him and those who only wanted to see him finally buried--all mourned him. [24]

* * *

---

24 Jose Hermano Saraiva

176

Continuing, Marco said, "After two years, Salazar removed more restrictions on foreign investment. A new Holiday Inn opened in Lisbon. Eventually, they asked me to be part of the initial hotel management team. I moved back to discover that my friend, Carlos, had been killed in a freak accident in Mozambique."

"Salazar was getting old. He ruled since 1932. In the 1960's, he finally began to allow limited foreign investment. I became one of the new technocrats in the blossoming hospitality industry."

"Where are your sister and mother?" Tomas asked.

"My sister, Teresa, married and lives in Porto now. My mother still lives with Luisa, my grandmother, in Sao Joao."

"So you don't know if your father is dead or alive?" inquired Tomas.

"No, we've never gotten any information about him."

Tomas was getting progressively more curious and asked, "What about Marta? How does she fit into the picture?"

"Marta's father was an officer in the army and he was stationed in Angola. He died from Yellow Fever while still in Africa. Marta became quite bitter. She blames the dictatorship for her father's death. She joined the resistance. She is a longtime friend and I've pledged to help her survive."

Tomas asked, "Are you part of the resistance?"

Marco looked around, carefully scrutinizing the people nearby and distant. Then he quietly answered, "Yes, but you must never have this conversation again in public. Even the telephones are not secure. Promise me never to talk about the regime unless we are absolutely alone."

"I understand, I think," Tomas whispered.

That night, Marco and Tomas walked home. Tomas had tremendous empathy for Marco because of his dramatic life events.

David Marty

After they undressed, Tomas just held Marco under the comforter. They didn't have sex that night; the moment was too somber. They fell asleep with Tomas' arms wrapping around Marco's strong chest. Tomas had the wildest dreams. He dreamt that he and Marco were at the nude beach under the sheets. At that moment, when the other men showered them with sperm, Tomas woke from his own sticky wet dream.

XXXVI

The End of an Era

Tomas thought about his father and knew that he would continue to try to find the true story of Tomas. In a dream, Tomas saw his father paying a friend to go to Portugal and spy on Tomas. His father, Paul, would figure out a way to finance such a plan on his always-short budget. Tomas always felt that his father had difficulty accepting him because of his sensitivity and disinterest in manly games and sports. He could remember his father dragging him to the tennis courts to get him to firm up his masculinity. Tomas hated tennis and always spent most of his time chasing balls. He was usually unable to connect with them.

Tomas arrived in Lisbon just after Salazar's death and funeral. He had no ideas of what a dictatorship was or what affect it had on the general population. After the birthday night with Marco, Tomas began to realize he could play an important role in spreading information between resistance groups. Tomas was becoming conversational in Portuguese. Yet, being an American, he could always deny knowing the language if detained. The government was most afraid of communism. They wouldn't immediately connect a young American with a revolutionary change of government. Tomas wanted a role that could highlight his talents of intelligence, capability, artistry and bravery. He was determined to get involved in the revolution and prove to his father that he had what it took to be a "real man."

On subsequent visits to the market, Tomas stood closer to Marta so he could overhear the conversation she had with the vendors. Marta also taught English as a second language and used her classes to allow resistance members to come together for planning meetings. Many of the market conversations were about these meetings, where and what day and what time. He learned which vendors were to be trusted and which were suspect.

Tomas also learned the resistance spread throughout Portugal and did not only include Lisbon. For some time, there had been incidents of civil disobedience and planned disruptions of government programs to try to strain the Salazar government. These incidents needed planning and coordination in order to be effective. He also became aware that the gay men and all women had a big stake in the overthrow of an archaic and repressive government.

XXXVII

The Detective

Tomas was becoming fluent in Portuguese and was a quick learner of the transit system. He tested himself by listening to a name of a place and then seeing how he could get there the easiest way. Sometimes names would throw him and he'd have to look them up on the map. Tomas also built a strong friendship with Marta and felt honored when she asked him to accompany her to her language classes/resistance meetings. Women rarely walked alone on the streets at night and Tomas felt like her bodyguard when she asked him to accompany her.

Tomas learned early-on how to get to the Holiday Inn and sometimes met Marco there for siesta lunch. It was a fun diversion from wandering the city. Marco would find an unoccupied room so that he and Tomas could engage in secret sex. It was awesome to cavort on a new and different bed and it was fun to lay naked joined at the groin over siesta. Marco made sure that the housekeeper cleaned up after them leaving the room pristine and spotless.

One day in December, Tomas left their home and took the tram to the Alfama section of Lisbon. This area was the oldest part of the city; the devastating destruction from the earthquake in the eighteenth century spared Alfama. Many of the buildings had not changed much since then. Tomas loved the Alfama. Alfama was a step back into the centuries. Women still hung laundry out the windows where the clothes fluttered above the streets like colored flags. Everything had a light dust on it but was generally sunlight clean. The neighborhood was stratified. It appeared that the wealthier people lived near the top of the hill. Below, there were shops and offices. Tomas always wondered about some of the raised thresholds and concluded that they needed to be high in order to let rainwater divert back into the streets. His favorite bookstore required him to step almost knee high to enter the premises.

Tomas' bookstore often carried rare books in English. He loved to spend time reading. Occasionally he even bought a book. Tomas was just leaving the store. He was in a hurry to catch the next tram to take him to the Holiday Inn for a rendezvous with Marco. In his hast to be prompt, he rushed around a corner and literally bumped into a middle-aged woman carrying packages. The packages fell from her arms and scattered over the cobblestone. The woman nearly toppled to the ground as well; but the strong arms of Tomas propped her up.

"Desculpe," Tomas said as politely as he knew how.

The woman was startled but stood silent. She didn't understand Portuguese.

Tomas finally realized that she was an American tourist. "I'm so sorry, are you ok? Can I help you with your things?" Tomas said in English.

"Yes, I think that I'm alright, thank you. I was trying to find my way to the tram that I can take back to my hotel."

"Maybe I can help you," Tomas said. "My name is Tomas. Where are you trying to get to?"

"I am Betty McGivney. I'm here with my husband Alfred and we're staying at the Holiday Inn."

"What a coincidence. That's where I'm headed. Please come along with me. I'd be most happy to show you the way."

"That's a lovely red sweater you're wearing," Betty concluded.

"Thank you. I bought it right here in Lisbon. It's made in Portugal."

Once seated on the tram, the two sat side by side and began to talk. For Tomas, it was the first American he'd talked to since early in his hitchhiking days. Betty enjoyed talking and she told him that she and her husband arrived in Lisbon just a few days earlier. For Betty, the trip was a second honeymoon on their twenty-fifth wedding anniversary.

"What do you think of Lisbon so far? You probably just got here and haven't seen much," inquired Tomas.

"So far I feel Lisbon is a very enchanting and romantic city. It seems sort of feudal and antiquarian," she responded.

Tomas added with some laughter, "There are certainly a lot of old treasures in this city. Why did you choose Lisbon for your anniversary?"

"My husband is a detective. He got a job offer to come to Lisbon to look up a son of his client to see how he's doing."

"Oh, I see. " Tomas immediately thought of his father and wondered if Paul had actually paid a detective to locate him. He wouldn't put it past him but decided it was probably all a coincidence.

"You have a Midwest accent," Tomas mentioned.

"Yes. We are from Minneapolis, Minnesota. This is the most exotic place I've ever been. It has such a fairy tale look with so much romanticism."

"I find it has an elegant quaint feeling to it. People are generally very friendly and helpful even though many do not speak other languages," Tomas replied. Then he added a caution, "Make sure you don't go walking alone after dark. It isn't always safe for women."

It took only a few stops before the tram pulled up to the Holiday Inn. Both Betty and Tomas stepped down to the street. Tomas took Betty's arm and hustled her into the hotel lobby. Betty was happy to be at home base once again. Tomas knew she would be all right from there, excused himself and went off to find Marco.

XXXVIII

Discoveries

Tomas met up with Marco at the hotel. He told Marco, "You'll never believe this but I think my father has hired a private detective to find me. I'm sure I met the detective's wife today and rode the tram with her to the hotel. They're staying here!"

Marco sat processing this piece of information. "Your father must be very concerned about you if he'd go to that much trouble."

"My father is very orthodox and is not supportive of homosexuality. Dad needs tight control and I've abandoned many of his most cherished principles. I'm a little scared to meet this detective but my father can't make me go back."

Marco consoled him by saying, "You have to live your own life. Maybe we can influence this detective positively so that he can go back and talk to your father in a caring way."

"I know I can't run away and disappear but I'd sure like to."

"Let's cross that bridge when it gets built."

The next day, Tomas was having coffee at the restaurant around the corner from his house. He wore his red sweater to warm the

David Marty

chill in the air. He was feeling confident that Marco would be supportive of his new life. As he chose a morning pastry, he looked over and noticed an older man with dark glasses. The man seemed to be studying him. Tomas couldn't help but notice that the man seemed to blush even though the sun was not hitting him in the face. The man kept staring. Tomas could swear he saw a rise in his baggy pleated pants just under the zipper. The man abruptly lowered the newspaper he was reading to cover his crotch. Tomas concluded his own beauty drew the man to him. He'd noticed that scrutiny before. Tomas felt this stranger was mentally undressing him with a stare. It seemed obvious the man was getting sexually aroused over Tomas. Tomas loved it.

There were only a handful of other patrons and Tomas wondered why the man focused on him so intently. The man was nothing to look at, older, stocky and balding. Tomas didn't get the return radar that Alfred was gay. It was impossible to read his eyes through the sunglasses.

Alfred nervously approached the table where Tomas sat. He asked, "Do you perhaps speak English?"

"Yes, I do," Tomas replied in his Midwest accent.

Then Alfred continued, "I am trying to find this address." He pulled out his notes and showed Tomas the address.

"Well, that's actually my address. Why were you trying to find my house?"

"Is your name Thomas?

"Yes, it is."

"My name is Alfred. I'm a friend of your father, Paul, and a private detective. He's been worried about you and sent me to look you up to see how you're doing." Alfred's penis had deflated and blood began to filter back into his brain.

"I've been expecting you actually," Tomas said. "I believe I met your wife, Betty, yesterday coming back from Alfama. I helped her get back to the hotel she said you were staying at. My boyfriend Marco *(there, he finally admitted it already)*, works there and I also work there on occasion."

"Your father wants to make sure that you're alright and not in any danger."

"I am very fine, safe, well-fed and happy. I'm living with my friend Marco and he is a vice president of Holiday Inn, Lisbon. Our standard of living is above average. I've been marginally involved with the resistance to the government here. There are times this is dangerous, but I'm well placed and volunteer in mostly non-threatening ways."

Tomas noticed Alfred's penis swell again as he looked at Tomas' dark brown eyes and full sensuous lips. Then he asked, "Tomas are you a homosexual?"

"Yes, I guess I am; though I prefer to be called gay. I think men are sexy."

Again fully erect, Alfred attempted to blunt his feelings. "I know that your father doesn't approve of homosexuality, what do you want me to tell him about that part of your life?"

"Why don't you and your wife come to our house and have a Portuguese dinner tomorrow. You'll be more able to observe our life and it may help you to find answers for my dad."

"That's a generous offer that I shouldn't pass up. I'll talk to Betty and if she agrees, we'll plan on showing up. What would be a good time?"

"People eat late here; I think seven would be a good starting point."

"Ok, we'll see you at seven if Betty agrees; otherwise I'll call to cancel."

David Marty

Tomas was relieved and apprehensive at the same time. He hadn't cleared any of this with Marco and Marta needed to be involved. Tomas called Marco at work. He mentioned that he'd met the detective already and not knowing what to do; he'd invited the wife and the detective to dinner the next evening.

Marco initially thought Tomas had made a huge blunder. Yet, as he thought about it, he decided maybe this would be a good way to leave the detective with a positive impression. He told Tomas to get a hold of Marta and come up with a menu worthy of the Portuguese culture.

Tomas called Marta and explained the situation to her. Always the optimist, she started right away to plan a traditional menu. Marta hadn't made it for a long time but the occasion seemed to deserve Cozido a Portuguesa, a hearty boiled dinner. For appetizers, she decided to make cod balls with a few varieties of cocktail sardines, cheeses and wine. Marta was anxious to display a gracious Portugal as well.

Amid all the thought of preparation for the dinner, Tomas had time to contemplate Alfred and Betty. He knew that Alfred was happily married with children. His encounter that morning divulged an Alfred with a renewed sexual appetite. Tomas had seen firsthand how Alfred's testosterone skyrocketed upon gazing at him. Tomas was going to make it a point to quiz Betty about the afternoon. He suspected that Alfred would be inspired to make love to Betty all the while fantasizing about Tomas.

Not all the preparations for the Portuguese dinner were finished before the guests arrived. Marta had tidied the place up and brought in fresh flowers. She was still busy frying cod balls when the bell rang. She wasn't accustomed to guests showing up exactly on time. It was considered more polite to

188

be about a half-hour late. A well-dressed Tomas greeted the McGivney's at the front door. He led them to the living room and offered each of them a glass of wine. Marco suddenly appeared from the master bedroom and Tomas introduced him to the couple.

Alfred understood what Tomas saw in Marco. He was handsome in an Aryan way with light brown, short curly coarse hair. He was dressed in expensive leisure clothes and he wore them well. He had broad shoulders and a classically chiseled physic. His strong legs supported his upright posture. He resembled King Charles of Portugal that Alfred saw in some 1910 photos.

Betty was easily charmed; she blushed when Marco took her hand in his, and gave it a kiss. Alfred liked the firm handshake. Then Marta appeared with a platter of cheese and bread and a bottle of white wine. Setting things down on the coffee table, she refilled empty glasses and returned to the kitchen to fetch the fish balls.

The conversation roamed around Lisbon and Portugal. All the rich history enthralled Betty. Alfred tried to insert questions into the conversation about employment and finances. He could easily conclude that Marco was nowhere near poverty. He also could see that Marco was sincere in his promise to take care of Tomas. Alfred was a little jealous of Marco that he could find and score such a beautifully sensual man like Tomas.

By the end of the night, Betty was getting tipsy. Tomas took her aside to ask, "How was your afternoon yesterday?"

She confided, "You know, I've never seen Alfred so full of fun and so amorous. Then she added in a whisper, "We made love longer than we've ever done before and I told him, if it's Portugal, we'll have to travel more often."

David Marty

Betty had spilled the beans and Alfred was getting sleepy. Marco called a cab for them and everyone said goodbye. The evening had gone well.

The McGivneys were gone, Marta bade farewell, and Tomas and Marco soon retired to the bedroom. Tomas was more appreciative of Marco than ever before. They undressed and lay with their arms wrapped around one another. Tomas kissed Marco sweetly, and then traced the outline of his lips with his tongue. Tomas moved so that he was on top of Marco. They slowly warmed their bodies with the friction of frottage. Each with huge pulsing matching erections and body heat sent them into an ethereal reality. They shot their loads in synchrony and continued to writhe in the sticky goo of their sperm. They giggled as they assessed their "depravity." Tomas couldn't understand why such feelings of wonderment should be wasted on "deviants." Both men had witnessed farm animals experiencing similar pleasures. It was beautifully natural and wonderfully fulfilling and exhilarating.

Tomas knew that Alfred and Betty would soon be heading home. He hoped that Marco and he had made a favorable impression on them. He sensed that Alfred was much more tolerant than his conservative father was. Tomas made every effort to show the detective that his liaison with Marco was safe, happy and full of promise for his future. Tomas predicted that he wouldn't have such a happy life if he returned home. He decided that Alfred must have felt renewed and inspired in the idea of sex as a therapy rather than just for procreation. Tomas hoped Betty would gladly share his newfound sensuality.

190

Liberating Tomas

01-01-71

Dear Tom,

Happy New Year. Your father has heard from the detective that he sent to learn more about your new life. Of course, he can't understand why you've chosen a different and sinful life-style. He's angry and upset. I personally don't believe it's a matter of choice though. I love you and I'm trying to understand the whole thing. I have searched the scriptures and haven't found any direct condemnation from Christ. I believe that some people are especially chosen to teach the rest of us how we can be more loving and accepting, just as Jesus was. Your father needs some time now and it helps that there is a long distance between the two of you. I'll always love you as an especially sensitive son. Please keep in touch and let me know if there's anything I can do to help you with your life. I don't want you to shut me out. Let me work on your father. *Love, Mom*

XXXIX

A Member of the Resistance

Tomas and Marta had become such very good friends. Tomas went along with her to the markets and accompanied her to her classes and resistance group meetings. After meeting many of the other people from the resistance, Marta explained to Tomas that one group that she had difficulty reaching was the gay men. Many of the younger men were off the radar because they didn't like conscription. Lots of artists and gays had immigrated to Paris, which boasted it was the second largest city of Portuguese population in the world after Lisbon. Tomas knew French. He was rapidly learning Portuguese. He was a natural in cementing a revolutionary bond to the gay/artsy crowd. Marta encouraged Tomas to hang around at the parties and clubs frequented by gays. Of course, Tomas was more than willing to play this role.

As 1970 moved into 1971, Tomas entrenched himself into the somewhat down-low gay culture. Salazar had never been married nor was there ever any romantic woman in his life. He might have been celibate like a member of clergy. Perhaps he was deeply closeted. In any case, he had a disdain for gays that sometimes translated to dispersals, arrests and punishments.

192

Tomas for many months remained steadfastly faithful to Marco. He was so grateful to have an older role model that he could imitate. Marco taught him how men could be sexually tender with one another. Marco also projected confidence and acceptance over wide issues of homosexuality. Marco had neither chosen nor questioned his sexual preferences. Marco taught him that homosexuality could be beautiful without any consideration of sinfulness. Love was love and sharing sexuality with another man was wildly fulfilling. Their chemistry was a superb match. Male heterosexuals could never appreciate such intimacy.

After several months absorbing whatever he could from Marco, Tomas began to wonder what casual sex with other men might be like. Marco and Tomas had a small circle of friends. Most of Marco's friends seemed older and more traditional. However, one young man, Will, stood out. Tomas and Will were around the same age. Will was English but lived with an older Portuguese man. Tomas admired his fine physique and sometimes at one of the underground clubs, he had the opportunity to dance with him. Marco noticed the fascination Tomas held for Will. He observed but tried not to discourage their times together. Marco knew Will's older friend, Lucas, and sometimes the four of them went out together.

One time, when Will and Tomas were alone for a brief moment, Will asked Tomas if he knew about the park. Tomas didn't know anything about the park.

"What park are you talking about?" Tomas inquired.

"I'm talking about the Botanical Gardens; you've never heard anything about it?"

"No, I have no idea what you're talking about."

David Marty

"Maybe Marco doesn't want you to know of it, but after midnight, it is a meeting place for gays who want to share sex but don't have anywhere else to go."

"Really? You mean guys meet up there to have sex?"

"Yes, but what's so fun is when the weather's warm, men get naked and have anonymous sex in the bushes."

"Wow, I'd love to see that."

"It's always at nighttime and it's difficult to see unless you are right in the middle of it. I should mention that the police know it is a hangout and occasionally raid it. People can get arrested if not careful."

"So you've been there?"

"Yes, a few times. I've had fun sex there. One can hardly see who you're playing with but that's part of the intrigue."

Tomas was getting erect thinking about it and asked Will, "Is there a particular area where men congregate?"

"Some night that Marco is busy working, a weekend is best, I should take you there and you'll see."

Tomas' curiosity was making his mind wander to crazy places. He wanted to go with Will, but he was sure Marco wouldn't approve. He didn't want to keep secrets from Marco. Yet, because of his youth, he was anxious to explore a wider sexual freedom.

He told Will, "Keep me up on things and I'll call if there's ever a chance to sneak off to the park."

The fantasy of anonymous sex with other men sustained sex between Tomas and Marco at a fertile plain. Tomas thought about penetration by a naked stranger, outside in the warm night. He also thought about wrapping his lips around other men's penises when he was swallowing Marco. Marco even asked

194

what was going on that their sex had intensified. Fantasy fueled the sexual fires.

Several weeks later, Marco announced to Tomas, "I have to stay overnight at the hotel tomorrow. I will not be home 'til sunup."

"What's going on at work that you need to stay?"

"They're putting in a new elevator and someone needs to supervise the workers. I thought I should volunteer."

"Tomorrow night is Friday night. I was hoping to go out dancing."

"That's fine. Maybe you can call and see if Will and Lucas are going and you could go with them."

"O.k. I will try it. I don't like going alone, without you."

Tomas was nervously anxious. If he went to the club with Will, they could spend part of the night at the Botanical Gardens. All day Tomas played with himself, stimulating his penis. He would bring himself just to the edge, and then back off. It would have only taken another few seconds sometimes but Tomas wanted to save his hormonal crescendo for later in the evening.

Tomas met Will at the club. Lucas wasn't there.

"Where's Lucas?" Tomas asked.

"He was tired. He gave me the keys to the Vespa and told me to enjoy myself." Will had a devilish look about him.

The two danced and had a few drinks. It was soon after midnight and just after they had danced a fourth song, Will nudged Tomas over to the side and said, "I think we should leave early and go to the park."

"Really, it's not too early/"

"It's early but it gets even seedier after the beginning."

"O.k. I'm ready then. Can you drive alright after drinking?"

David Marty

"Sure, Come on, let's go already."

Tomas hopped on the back of the scooter and put his arms around Will. Will's tight young body seemed even more erotic than Marco's did. Maybe it was just a good difference. They zoomed down a few streets and around Principe Real. They turned after the science museum and were on the north end of the gardens. A small parking area had plenty of room for the Vespa. There were a few other cars but many more people must have taken public transit.

Will led the way with Tomas close at his heels. A grove of towering Norfolk pines softened the quiet noises coming from under them. Tomas couldn't believe his eyes. Pine branches muted the moon, but he could see several dark shapes of men in various stages of undress. There was very little talk. There must have been at least twenty men. Many were stark naked. As he got closer, one man, quite young Tomas could see, was bent forward with his hands balanced on the grass as if hiking a football. There was a line of three or four quarterbacks waiting to penetrate the naked man.

Tomas wanted to move closer to the front of the line to touch the young man and his admirers and see the penetrations up close. Will pulled Tomas aside and cautioned him with whispers about etiquette. Tomas pulled his pants off and held them in his hands. Then he spotted a park bench and went over to sit on it. Tomas was sitting on his pants with his fingers wrapped around his penis, which was getting hard and springy. Two young men approached Tomas. One quickly kneeled down and began to lick Tomas' penis. Tomas thought about Marco and shooed him on. The other extended his penis to Tomas' mouth so that Tomas might taste him. Tomas refused the advance. The two seemed like twins and were completely naked. They each had

196

well sculpted bodies and strong hairy legs. The man who wanted Tomas to taste him had a beautifully rounded rear end that was baby skin soft. As Tomas tickled his scrotum, the man shot his load that launched yards away in the grass.

The second man, startled by the rejection, shot a huge load over Tomas' chest, which then dripped down toward his loins. Tomas returned to the young man impaled by successive penises. The line was gone now and one man was just finishing, driving a big load into the youth. Tomas moved to the man's head and kissed him sweetly on the lips. The man looked at Tomas and asked in Portuguese if Tomas would like to be the final episode. Tomas was flattered that the young man accepted him as Portuguese. Instead of following his hormones, he gently lifted the young man to a standing position and gave him a warm hug. Tomas decided that looking and watching was enough education for the night. He cherished the intimacy of Marco too much to ruin the relationship that was still so new.

About then, sirens started to wail and Will told Tomas, "We'd better get out of here. I'm sure it's the police."

They jumped on the Vespa and headed towards Marco's house. Will dropped Tomas off and left into the night. Exhilaration overtook Tomas from all the sexual attractions. He was grateful that he chose to deny penetration. He enjoyed the voyeurism but he was pleased with himself that he'd resisted involvement in an orgy of strangers. He would be much more receptive to Marco when he returned home. Unfulfilled fantasies spun through his head and he fell asleep with a dripping erection.

.Marco arrived home around six in the morning. He had a very long night and the new elevator had tested out well. He crept into the bedroom to find Tomas lying naked in the bed. Fending sleep, Tomas waited to feel Marco's hands on him and

David Marty

he obligingly lessened the grip on his hole. Marco felt the release and slowly yet fully penetrated the willing rectum. Tomas wandered in and out of dreamland reassured that he'd given Marco's erect penis its true home. Semen flooded his hole and Tomas thought about the young man who was repeatedly flooded. They both fell asleep joined together.

XL

The Beach

In early August, Marco came home from work with a big smile on his face. Tomas quizzed him, "OK, so what's going on that I should know?"

"You remember a while ago I told you that I'd like to show you the clothing optional beach on the ocean?"

"I remember very well. I was hoping that you'd bring the subject up again."

"I talked to another guy in corporate and he asked if I would take some time off. He's offered me a week at his villa on the beach. The same beach I used to go to with my friend, Carlos. I want you to get ready and pack for a week at Costa da Caparica!"

Tomas was surprised but said, "I can't wait, I've been thinking about it ever since you talked about it. I hoped that we'd go last summer but you never mentioned it. I'm really ready to go now."

"Well, get ready, we're leaving Saturday. I'll drive."

"I'd love to do the driving for you," Tomas replied.

"I guess it's ok. It doesn't really matter who drives."

Marco was finally going to show Tomas the clothing optional beach that he'd heard so much about.

David Marty

Marco found the suitcase and placed it on the floor near the foot of the bed. Every day for three days, the suitcase started filling up. Tomas asked Marco if he could buy a new swimsuit. Marco answered, "You don't really need one but maybe it's a good idea if you take one along. I'm bringing one and I'll buy you one to take along."

When Marco came home the next day, he had a small box wrapped with a bow on it. He presented it to Tomas. Tomas wondered if it was jewelry because the box was so tiny. He quickly unwrapped the box and pulled out a beautiful cobalt blue men's bikini. It was barely big enough to enclose Tomas' penis and left his beautiful buttocks fully exposed.

"Is this actually legal?" Tomas murmured

"It looks fabulous on you," Marco responded as Tomas tried it on.

They went to bed early on Friday night to get a head start on Saturday. Tomas drove the flashy convertible sport car with exuberance. The drive was about two and a half hours. Marco knew the way and Tomas listened for directions. They soon pulled up to a newer condominium facing the sea. Tomas bolted out of the car dragging the single suitcase.

"Wait for me, I've got the keys," Marco yelled, quickly following Tomas.

The "cottage" was ultra-modern and spotlessly clean. Tomas was in a hurry to get to the beach.

"Hold on a minute, we should eat some breakfast first and put on sun screen," Marco suggested.

The clothing optional part of the beach was on the far end and quite a long walk in the sand. When they finally arrived, Marco scouted the scenery and chose a large open space of sand to unfurl the sheet. Tomas rushed to the water's edge and put

200

Liberating Tomas

his foot in the water. It was a little cool even in August. Marco couldn't hide his pride at seeing Tomas in a bikini in the outdoor lighting.

Tomas returned to the sheet and asked Marco, Is it safe to swim here?"

"Of course, but always face the waves to know when the high rollers are pounding through."

A small picnic basket contained cheese, bread and wine, all that they'd need for a little while. Marco organized his space as another young man approached and began to set up his space nearby. Marco observed the stranger. He was dumfounded. He could've sworn that the new man was a mirror image of Tomas. Even the man's bathing suit was identical to the one he'd given Tomas except the color was yellow.

Tomas interrupted Marco's astonishment to ask what had garnered his utmost attention. Then Tomas looked to where Marco's fixed eyes focused and discovered his twin. It was eerie to see oneself almost as if looking in a mirror. Tomas stared at the young man seeing the same full lips, the lighter hair, the same physique and body structure and the same skin, even down to the exact same moles in the same areas.

Marco was somewhat unnerved by it all. How could there be another man as beautiful as Tomas? Marco wondered if the man was Portuguese or a different nationality. Tomas went to Marco and asked, "Do you see that guy? I swear he could be my twin brother!"

"Indeed he is exactly similar to you except for some skin tone coloring. In a little while when we all get settled, I'm going to talk to him and find out more."

Marco and Tomas began to get comfortable and each pulled off the swimsuit that they arrived in. They laid supine close to

201

each other. The warm sun was heating their bodies and it didn't take long for the warmth to reach their genitals. Marco looked at Tomas and watched his penis flair in the afternoon sun. What a beautiful sight.

Eyes wandering, Marco glanced to the stranger and watched the young man who was now naked and reveling in the warmth by sprouting his own erection. Marco turned his attention back to Tomas, whose penis was dancing in the sunlight. He brought his right hand to Tomas' penis and gently traced the organ with his fingers.

The stranger quietly observed the two feeling a little jealous because he didn't have a partner. He abruptly stood up, with a magnificent hard-on, walked to the sea, and gradually disappeared under the waves.

Tomas decided to follow the man, watching for clues on how to swim in an ocean. Once waist deep, he plunged into the sea. The surf was mild and swimming in salt water was easier than in fresh. Tomas swam out to where he could just touch bottom and bobbed up and down with the waves.

The stranger was swimming further out. When he saw Tomas enter the water, he gradually worked his way toward him. Then, to the surprise of Tomas, the young man spoke to him in English.

"How are you today?"

"I'm fine, and yourself?"

"Very good, here. May name is Ben. What's your name?"

"I'm Tomas. My friend's name is Marco."

"Are you Portuguese?"

Marco is Portuguese, I'm American, but I've been living here for a few years."

"I am Swiss. I'm traveling around Europe and decided to go swimming here."

Liberating Tomas

"That's interesting. I 'm part Swiss. I can't help seeing a resemblance in you."

"I noticed that right away too. Do the two of you play around?"

"We haven't done that yet. However, there's a first time for everything isn't there? I'm getting chilled. I'll go warm up and talk with Marco."

Tomas easily got out of the water and ran to the sheet where Marco was sitting. "You'll never guess. The man's name is Ben and he's Swiss," Tomas eagerly informed him.

"Oh, that's why there is such a strong resemblance," Marco conceded. Then Marco startled Tomas to ask, "Do you want to play with him?"

"I think it'd be a lot of fun, but I wouldn't want to play with him alone."

During their conversation, Ben sprang out of the water and dripping wet he made his way to his own sheet. Marco glanced at the glistening young Ben and then back to Tomas. Then Marco got up and walked confidently toward Ben. As he approached he said, "Hello Ben, my name is Marco, Would you be interested in joining us for the afternoon?"

A big smile gave the answer before Ben replied, "Why yes, that is so kind of you to offer."

Ben moved his sheet over to where Marco and Tomas lay. As Ben settled in, Marco reached over to trace the outlines Ben's erect nipples. Tomas watched with some jealousy. Soon, jealousy, incest, taboos, narcissism, morality and doubt evaporated like ether. The three explored one another stimulating and receiving each other's touch. The warm sun and the moist ocean air added to the sensuality. Each sculpted man freely engaged all the tender sensory and motor nerves. It felt as if they were on fire.

203

David Marty

Tomas was mesmerized. He couldn't tell if his penis was inflated. It felt like every cell of his body was pumped up on hormones. Exhilaration gave way to curiosity. The three men had entered a private domain of shear lust. It seemed so odd to lick Ben's toes and realize they were identical to the toes of his own self. Tomas couldn't get enough of Ben and mentally merged with his double.

This went on for over a half-hour. Others on the beach were getting a free show and yet the three men continued to cavort. With a small crowd growing larger, Marco suggested, "Let's go back to the villa and really get to business."

They walked the long beach to the lake house. As soon as they entered, they removed their suits and immediately resumed their naked explorations. It was hot inside the house and soon there was a pile of sweaty men. The orgy went on with each penis being mouthed and every anus impaled. Trying to hold back, the young men had multiple orgasms. Finally, even their youth didn't prevent them from becoming exhausted as they fell asleep in a tight clump.

Marco woke first and opened a window to mix fresh air to the smells of sweat and sperm. Tomas stirred and looked over to see Ben still sporting an erection. Tomas cleaned Ben's penis with his tongue, waking him. Then all three moved to the big shower to rinse.

Ben had some evening plans and excused himself. After he left, Marco hugged Tomas saying, "I think I got the best deal."

Tomas was satisfied that Marco was still the loyal friend he depended on.

The following morning, Tomas and Marco walked the beach scouting for Ben. He was nowhere to be found. Tomas even wondered if the whole incident was just an illusion. Marco reassured him that indeed it was splendidly real.

204

Liberating Tomas

08-13-72

Dear Mom and Dad,

It's been some time since I wrote last. I've been working and learning Portuguese. I'm not fully employed and have extra time to do other things. I've decided that I should get more involved with the revolution that is happening here. They told me that the insurgents could really use an expert communicator to make the disparate groups more unified. I've been given a huge responsibility to relay information not only in Portugal, but also in France. There is a large young Portuguese population in Paris that want to aid the resistance fighters. I'm joining the resistance so that I can have real purpose to my life and contribute to the future of Portugal, which I have come to love. I will be protected because of my U.S. citizenship, so don't worry. However, feel free to pray for me.

Love always,   Tomas

XLI

Triumph of Revolution

After Salazar's death, Marcelo Caetano solidified his power. Because of its anti-communist stance, NATO tolerated the undemocratic government. The economy of Portugal and its colonies was growing well above the European average in 1974. Banned labor unions and unenforced minimum wage policy ruled. Oddly, the one union that successfully formed before Salazar's death was that of the Fado musicians. Fado also allowed women to join the union, which struck an insulting blow to Salazar's belief that women should stay in the home.

The left winged Armed Forces Movement (MFA) initially was born out of disgruntled soldiers and their superiors who opposed the colonial wars. They formed a conspiracy to overthrow the government by military coup. [25]

Tomas was an important communication link between the parties of the MFA and the resistance. The man in charge of the MFA was General Antonio Spinola. His wife had a German mother, Gertrude. Years earlier, circumstances led Gertrude to seek medical care from Marco's father, Werner, and the two became friends.

---

25 Jose Hermano Saraiva-paraphrase

Because Tomas knew French, Marta again encouraged him to go to Paris. Tomas gladly accepted the new role and was soon on the midnight train headed to Paris to get support and contributions. Crossing the borders was scary. Portugal was wary of citizens abandoning their country. Tomas posed as the American that he was and authorities never detained him. Spain's border guards were even more cryptic. His passport proved to be invaluable for getting through without incident.

Tomas met with several expatriates and helped plan many successful fund raising events in Paris. He resisted the many attempts at personal sexual exploitation and took his job very seriously. Tomas spent two weeks in Paris. By the end of his visit, he relayed several thousands of dollars to Portugal's underground.

Tomas was now intimately engaged in the resistance. He often took Marta's place at the market to notify friends of meetings and scheduled acts of disobedience. He usually wore his red sweater to reassure others in the resistance of his loyalty. Occasionally, authority stopped him and asked for his papers. Upon seeing that he was an American, they let him go right away. Tomas was happy that he had a helpful and meaningful assignment.

07-01-73
Dear Son,

Happy Birthday. I'm writing this to let you know that I am quite proud that you are engaging in the Portuguese culture. I've been struggling with the knowledge of your homosexuality. I know you've told your mother that you think it's all about God's plan and not a choice. I know you're smart and I know that you'd never choose a lifestyle that was only based on sex. Secretly I've known since you were very young that you were different from

my other sons. You have a love of freedom and art that is now global. Please be careful in your espionage exploits. Revolutions can easily become violent and you could be hurt or killed. I have come to love you because you are my son, even though I might not ever understand homosexuality. I really wish the best for you and we will be following what's going on in Portugal although it is hard to get much information here. Please be careful. I will be praying for the best outcome.
Love, Dad

XLII

End Game

The signal to the start of the revolution was to be by music. Tomas travelled to many resistance meetings in and near Lisbon to tell the various factions of the resistance to listen to their radios for specific songs in the evening. In late March 1974, an assignment for Tomas became the challenging job of informing the resistance people who lived on the other side of the Tagus about the signals and plans. He needed to cross the military blockade that oversaw ferry traffic.

Tomas wore his red sweater and had a small leather satchel. He walked past a row of soldiers who gave him questioning glances. One of the soldiers broke from his companions and approached Tomas. He shouted out, "PARE." Tomas heard the soldier demanding him to stop but proceeded ahead anyway.

The soldier caught up with Tomas and brought him to a stop. Then he asked Tomas for his passport. Tomas kept saying in English, "I don't speak Portuguese." The uniformed man was intimidating but Tomas realized at that moment that his sexual preferences were exhilarated when gazing at men in uniform. The soldier scrutinized his American passport. Attempting to speak English, he said, "Your passport is expired. I cannot let you board the ferry."

David Marty

Tomas' assignment was to board and bring critical information to the east side of Portugal. Tomas pleaded with him to let him board. He would tend to his outdated passport at another time. Tomas worked hard to sway the soldier, but was unsuccessful. The soldier's instructions had been to be on the lookout for a boy in a red sweater. The soldier wasn't sure if this was a coincidence, or if he'd captured the true resistance communicator.

To get out of his predicament, Tomas decided that he was willing to flirt with this young stooge. Tomas smiled broadly and seemed to recognize a new gleam in his captor's eyes. Tomas motioned the man to follow him in to a restroom at the pier. The man complied. He followed Tomas into a large stall and removed his rifle from his shoulder. Tomas put his finger to his mouth to exact silence. Then he slowly started to undress the man from the waist down. By the time he got to the underclothes, the man's penis was at full attention. Tomas first nibbled on the foreskin, then swallowed the thick shaft all the way to the base. The man cupped Tomas' head with his hands and pressed his penis as deep as it could go into his mouth. This was the biggest penis Tomas had ever put in his mouth, even bigger than Marco was. He tried not to gag. It didn't take very long and soon the moaning military man was erupting volumes into the mouth of Tomas. Tomas savored the flavors and swallowed the last drop. It felt powerful to have a soldier share his DNA with him so intimately. The soldier was somewhat flushed but after Tomas cleaned him with his tongue, he dressed. The man warned Tomas that he must get his passport in order because the next guard may not be as considerate. Then he turned and left.

Tomas boarded the ferry and was on the other side of the Tagus before nightfall. He met with the head organizer of the

Liberating Tomas

resistance east of Lisbon and told him that broadcast clues would play on the radio when the revolution was getting started.

Tomas said, "Listen carefully for a Paulo de Carvalho song. This will be a clue for the MFA to be on alert. When the radio plays a song by Zeca Afonsa within several days, the revolution will be starting. You must spread this information to as many in the underground as you can."

The role of the resistance on the other side of the Tagus was to detain soldiers and disrupt traffic so that the military dictators couldn't rally their forces from other parts of Portugal.

On 6 April 1974, the first song by Paulo de Carvalho played to alert rebel captains and soldiers to put final touches on the coup. The resistance fighters were also listening for that cue. On 25 April, at 12:20 AM, Radio Renascenca broadcast the song by Zeca Afonsa, a folk artist much like Woody Guthrie and Joan Baez. He had previously been forbidden airtime from Portuguese radio by the regime. It was that signal, by which MFA announced the revolution's beginning and the takeover of strategic points of power. Marta, Tomas, and Marco had been listening to the radio intently for a month. They felt confident that they'd succeeded in preparing their friends for the starting day of the revolution.

By morning, thousands of Portuguese took to the streets mingling with MFA insurgents and offering them support. At the Lisbon flower markets, carnations were in season and many people, invested in freedom, placed red carnations into the gun barrels of the defending soldiers. Marta, Tomas and Marco brought armfuls of carnations and placed them stem by stem into automatic weapons pointed at them. The Carnation Revolution only lasted a few hours. Caetano (the prime minister) and Americo Tomas fled to Brazil. Spinola took on the role of President of the

David Marty

Republic. He was also instrumental in immediately liberating the colonies and freeing most Portuguese political prisoners.

Not a word had surfaced about Marco's father, Werner, since 1956. With the specific help of Spinola's mother-in-law Gertrude, the release of Werner, a prisoner in Sao Tome, was swiftly completed. During the next several months, more than a million retournos also arrived from the many colonial outposts of Portugal. Many of them flooded Lisbon and began to live in previously abandoned buildings. Others reunited with family.

Marco returned to work the week following of the revolution. The foreign guests at the hotel were amazed at the historical involvement of so many people. Guest safety and welfare was always Marco's primary responsibility. There was an excitement of new hope and new freedoms. Portuguese people who were intrinsically tight-lipped about government were suddenly willing to lend their voices to the reforms that needed to be put in place. Cacophonous joy abounded.

05-15-74
Dear Son,

We read in the New York Times that the revolution in Portugal has happened. We are grateful of the swift success and that there was so little bloodshed. We both hope that you're ok. You should know that your father wept when he heard of the success and I'm sure he was crying because of your bravery and your involvement. We both love you very much. We hope to visit Portugal sometime soon and you're always welcome to come home for a break. You can even bring Marco if you'd like.
Love, Mom

XLIII

The Finale

Angela answered the telephone. It was Werner. He sounded weak and tired, but he told her he was working his way back from Sao Tome to meet her. She immediately called Marco who was ecstatic. His father, the most precious role model of his life, was alive.

Their reunion held in Sao Joao included Angela, her mother, Luisa, Teresa and her husband along with their extended family of friends and some former patients. It was a jubilant celebration full of kisses and hugs. Long tables heaped with a diverse spread of food welcomed guests. The slaughtered prize pig was roasted. Fruits and garden vegetables abounded. Wine flowed freely. Tomas was thrilled to be part of the revolution. Werner felt so fortunate to be back. He was proud of his son who never stopped his involvement in the resistance. Marco's endurance helped to buy Werner his freedom. Werner looked at Tomas and gave Marco an approving wink. He loved his son no matter what and was satisfied that Marco had a loving partner.

Tomas was genuinely moved that his own father was finally able to accept him and validate him, at least on some level. It was a good start. Tomas never intended to disappoint his father. Tomas celebrated the freedom of Portugal but much more

213

David Marty

intimately, he was simultaneously celebrating his own sexual liberation.

Women, gays, artists and poets, most of the poor, and those who had emigrated illegally, all would benefit from the Carnation Revolution. It would take several years before lasting reforms could change the backwardness of Salazar. Nevertheless, it was the beginning of true liberation, not just for Tomas and his sexuality, but also for all the people of Portugal and their future visitors. It was the new beginning of the modern era.

The End and a New Beginning